THE BEST

MISTAKE

MYSTERY

THE BEST MISTAKE MYSTERY

MYSTERY

THE GREAT MISTAKE MYSTERIES

sylvia mcnicoll

DUNDURN
TORONTO

Cover image: © Tania Howells
Printer: Webcom

Library and Archives Canada Cataloguing in Publication

McNicoll, Sylvia, 1954-, author
    The best mistake mystery / Sylvia McNicoll.

(The great mistake mysteries)

Issued in print and electronic formats.
ISBN 978-1-4597-3625-2 (paperback).--ISBN 978-1-4597-3626-9 (pdf).--
ISBN 978-1-4597-3627-6 (epub)

   I. Title.

PS8575.N52B473 2017   jC813'.54   C2016-903430-5
                                     C2016-903431-3]

1 2 3 4 5   21   20 19 18 17

Conseil des Arts du Canada Canada Council for the Arts Canadä ONTARIO ARTS COUNCIL CONSEIL DES ARTS DE L'ONTARIO an Ontario government agency un organisme du gouvernement de l'Ontario

We acknowledge the support of the **Canada Council for the Arts** and the **Ontario Arts Council** for our publishing program. We also acknowledge the financial support of the **Government of Ontario**, through the **Ontario Book Publishing Tax Credit** and the **Ontario Media Development Corporation**, and the **Government of Canada**.

The author would like to thank the Ontario Arts Council for its support through the Writer's Reserve Program.

Care has been taken to trace the ownership of copyright material used in this book. The author and the publisher welcome any information enabling them to rectify any references or credits in subsequent editions.

— *J. Kirk Howard, President*

The publisher is not responsible for websites or their content unless they are owned by the publisher.

Printed and bound in Canada.

VISIT US AT

dundurn.com | @dundurnpress | dundurnpress | dundurnpress

Dundurn
3 Church Street, Suite 500
Toronto, Ontario, Canada
M5E 1M2

For everyone who has ever walked a dog before but especially for the people who help me walk Mortie (aka Ping) and Worf (aka Pong): my grandchildren, Hunter, Fletcher, Finley, William, Jadzia, Violet, Desmond, and Scarlett

While the setting and some of the mistakes may be real, the kids, dogs, teachers, principals, custodians, and neighbours are all made up. If you recognize yourself or anyone else, you've clearly made a mistake. Good for you!

day one

THE GREAT MISTAKE

MYSTERIES

DAY ONE, MISTAKE ONE

At three o'clock in the afternoon, the fire alarm jangles. Mrs. Worsley's arms startle open like a bird's wings, but she quickly folds them back down across her chest, hiding her hands in her armpits. Her woolly eyebrows knit and her mouth purls.

"I've taught here for thirty years," she told us on the first day of school. "There is nothing you can do that will shock me."

But on day thirty, this alarm takes her by surprise. Drills are always planned, which can only mean one thing.

I leap from my seat, wave my arms, and shout, "Fire! Fire!"

No one moves.

Mrs. Worsley's left eye twitches as she reaches up to grab my shoulders — I'm taller than she is — and squeezes gently. "Stephen Noble, calm down."

Everyone stares. My face turns hot. Mistake number one of the day.

My mother says I read too much into things. That's what I've done with this fire alarm. Based on Mrs. Worsley's body language, I decided it was a real-life emergency and jumped to warn everyone. Now they're all snickering behind their hands or rolling their eyes at silly old Green Lantern, my nickname since grade four.

Back then at least I had a best friend, Jessie, who stood by me when I did goofy things, even when I dropped my jeans to change for gym and had boxers on instead of gym shorts. Of course, they were the Green Lantern specials that Mom brought back from England. Jessie told everyone that I had changed into my secret identity. None of the kids believed him.

"If that's the worst mistake you made all day, Stephen, you're rockin'," Mom had said on her phone the morning after the underwear thing. She works as a flight attendant, so she's away a lot. To make me feel better, she told me a story about how the pilot forgot to put the landing gear down that day and how that caused a belly landing and quite some damage.

"You could have been hurt," I told her.

"True, but I wasn't. Nobody was." She sighed. "Don't think so hard about things. By next week everyone will have forgotten about your Green Lantern incident."

Shows you what she knows. The nickname lingers on. Also my fear of airplane travel.

Yelling out "Fire! Fire!" may not have been as bad as dropping my drawers three years ago, but it's still the worst mistake for me today and I'm definitely not rockin'. On top of that, Jessie moved away over the summer. There will be no one to stick up for me later when everyone makes even more fun of me.

It started back in that grade four gym class and continues. It would be way easier to make a new friend if I were good at a team sport. If I were any good at soccer, Tyson and Bruno and me might be pals. Instead, I trip when I kick at the ball and let goals go by me. Because I'm tall and have long arms and legs, everyone expects me to be good at basketball, but I can't sink a basket. Or spike a volleyball. What I excel at isn't played at school: Wii bowling. I sigh. Jessie is a great Wii bowler, too.

Mrs. Worsley releases my shoulders and faces the rest of the kids. "Grade seven, line up quickly and quietly."

Renée's hand shoots up but Mrs. Worsley ignores her. I can't blame her. Renée's hand is always up. And if the teacher even looks her way, Renée's glittery glasses or hairband might blind her. Renée will keep waving her hand until Mrs. Worsley becomes hypnotized into answering her. And the teacher can never answer just one question. There's always another question and another till it turns into this big back and forth discussion. Which is why nobody wants Mrs. Worsley to call on Renée. It always slows everything down.

"Should we take our things?" Renée yells out when Mrs. Worsley continues to ignore her.

This time Princess Einstein has a point. In about fifteen minutes the final dismissal bell will ring.

Mrs. Worsley shakes her head. "No talking! Hurry!" She shoos us with her hands toward the door.

Everyone lines up.

"Renée, Stephen, you two go ahead and hold the doors."

She's pairing us up again like she's done from the beginning of school, as though she wants to keep us out of her hair. I understand giving Renée keep-busy work; otherwise, she'll question Mrs. Worsley to death. But me?

Of course, whenever we have to partner up, there's no Jessie, so Renée's pretty much my only choice, anyway, and where I'm super tall and bad at sports, Renée is super short and bad.

As we lead the way down the hall, I search for flames and sniff for smoke. Nothing.

"Hurry, Stephen!"

I hustle to catch up to Renée at our class's set of exit doors and slam my back into the remaining one to open and hold it in place.

"Nice job, Green Lantern," Tyson says as he passes through.

"Wearing your ring?" his friend Bruno asks.

"Sure is," Tyson says. "He put out the fire while we weren't looking."

Har de har har, I think.

The whole school pours out through three exits. Long streams of students spill over from the blacktop to the field.

Finally, when no one seems to be left inside the school, Renée and I let the doors shut behind us.

"Crazy to have a drill at the end of the day," Renée says. "Something has to be up."

Mrs. Worsley gives us the glare.

"Shh! We'll get a detention." Talking during a drill is a big no-no at our school. Still, I'm glad Renée thinks the same way I do. We walk together to the end of our line. I feel like a gawky giant next to shorty glitter girl.

Teachers begin to count the kids in their lines and, one by one, hold up their clipboards to signal to the principal, Mrs. Watier, that everyone is accounted for.

Mrs. Watier is new to our school and young and hip compared to Mrs. Worsley. She drives a black convertible TZX and wears tall black boots with everything, even jeans. Mrs. Worsley drives a beige, boxy car and wears white sneakers with all her clothes, skirts and dresses included. No jeans, not ever. Today, our cool principal paces and studies the rows of students, eyes narrowed.

All the clipboards go up. No students lost in this disaster.

No sirens wail, no fire trucks pull up. Maybe it's just a drill, after all. Mrs. Watier talks to each teacher, and after she chats with ours, our regular end-of-the-day bell rings and Mrs. Worsley dismisses us.

"But I don't have my agenda!" Renée protests.

"Never mind. Forget your homework for one night. Go straight home, please."

I squint at the school doors. If it's not a real fire, then why can't we go back in?

Mrs. Worsley is the queen of the agenda. Everything we do in class — tests, runs for cures, videos we watch, all the stuff we're supposed to do for homework, books or chapters to read, websites to browse, things we need to bring in, every gym or crazy hat or hair day, everything — she wants us to write it down and have our parents sign it so they know about it. "Never-minding" us about the agenda is a weird thing for her to do. I can't believe this is just a drill. She would make us write that in the agenda. Something way more serious has to be happening.

"Stephen, did you hear me?"

"Yes, Mrs. W."

"Then be on your way."

I have another important job starting today, so leaving right on time without homework would be very convenient if it weren't so suspicious. At the edge of the schoolyard, I turn to look back at the school and scan the building. I'm looking for a sign, a clue, something to let me know why Mrs. Worsley was so anxious to get rid of us.

DAY ONE, MISTAKE TWO

No agenda, no books, no homework — I should be dancing the happy zombie dance. But at home, I still wonder about that drill. I take a McIntosh from the fridge, wash it carefully, slice it into quarters, then eighths, and spread peanut butter over the pieces. Ahhh! The smoothness of the peanut butter calms me as I bite in. Too bad our school can't allow us to bring any for lunch. When I'm done, I slide my plate into the dishwasher, wash my face and hands, and brush my teeth triply long. If I meet someone along the way with a nut allergy, they should be fine.

Then I switch into my Noble Dog Walking sweatshirt and cargo pants. The shirt sports Dad's logo: a paw print with the word NOBLE over it and a dog bone underneath with DOG WALKING written inside. Dad used to be an air traffic controller, which is how he met Mom, but guiding airplanes stressed him too much, so he started this business because he says nothing calms you quite like walking a dog.

When Jessie left, I needed something to do; I've always wished I could have a pet, but we can't 'cause of Mom's allergies, so I asked if I could help. Dad liked the idea and he got me this uniform, which matches his exactly. Mom says we look like twins, but Dad's even taller than I am and keeps his hair cut really short to hide that he's losing it. Mine's black and shaggy, more like Mom's. But just like Dad, I use all the pockets in the cargo pants. There's one for everything I need:

Dog treats, the best ones in town 'cause Dad makes them from scratch — check.

Nobel Dog Walking business cards — check.

Poop 'n' scoop bags — check.

A ball to throw — check.

And the key to the Bennetts' house — check.

Ready to go, I head out the door again.

Dad has a bunch of dogs to walk during the late-afternoon time slot, so he's subcontracted the Bennetts' two to me. They're airline people, too, so they're away a lot, but they know me and trust me. Mrs. Bennett often carpools with Mom. Today's my first day on the job alone.

I walk the five houses down to the Bennetts'. When I head up the walkway, Ping, their scruffy Jack

Russell, barks his alert to the world. As he barks, he bounces up and down in front of the window like a … well … a ping-pong ball. *Rouw, rouw, rouw!*

Pong, their tall, slim greyhound, leans the top half of his body on the frame of the window and wags his long tail silently.

When I unlock the door and step inside, the dogs rush me, Ping leaping up and nipping at my pant leg, and Pong sidling strong and silent to push Ping out of the way.

"Down!" I call to the dogs.

Ping makes a lucky leap on to the pocket with my phone.

Blip, blip, blip, blip, blip, blip, blip!

Nuts. I didn't lock my phone. Ping just speed-dialed my father. Mistake two of the day. Now Dad will think I'm incompetent.

"Hello, Dad?" I say when he picks up. "Sorry. The dog jumped on the cellphone."

"Do you want to walk them one at a time?"

"No. We all have to get used to each other."

"Okay, then. Lock your phone."

"Doing that now. Bye."

Ping is still jumping.

"Sit!" I holler. Then I rattle the bag with Dad's legendary liver bites. Instantly, Ping sits and I snap his leash on. Pong sidesteps my grab for his collar while Ping circles, binding my legs.

Another rattle of the treats draws Pong close enough to snag, too. "There, now!"

Shuffling to the door loosens the noose around my ankles, and I step out to grab the handle. I gently sweep Ping away with my foot to open the door. The pair spring for the outdoors, but I yank them back so I can lock up.

And we're off — like a wagon pulled by a mismatched team, a horse and a pony. The sun shines bright this October afternoon, making the air just one notch warmer than crisp. The team drags me along the sidewalk toward Brant Hills, the park they love.

Ping snarls at Pong when he knocks him aside to get ahead. His snout wrinkles, his lips peel back, and his pink gums show. Nasty rabid raccoon snarl.

"Stop!" I command.

He snaps at Pong's long toes and scoots ahead. When Pong lifts his leg on a lamppost, Ping doubles back to salute it, too.

School was dismissed about a half an hour ago, and Mr. Ron, the crossing guard, must be about to walk home when he calls out to me from the corner. "First day on the job?"

I nod. I gave him our business card yesterday and told him about Ping and Pong.

"You gotta show them two who's boss." He points the stop sign in his hand at the dogs. "Give those leashes a good yank."

"I'll try, Mr. Ron." I don't want to look like a bad dog walker, so I tug back hard.

"Yup, yup, yup," he agrees with my efforts. Stuffed behind a yellow and orange safety vest, Mr. Ron's belly leads the way as he starts across the street, one gigantic hand acting as a safety gate in front of us, the other holding up his sign. We're halfway across when a Volkswagen Beetle roars around the corner. Ping lunges to attack the noise. I yank back hard, as Mr. Ron pushes me along with his shovel-like hands. The dogs tumble after me, landing on the sidewalk. The car doesn't even brake. Its tires brush by Ping's back leg.

DAY ONE, MISTAKE THREE

Ping's bark rises in pitch.

"Shhh! Ping, you're okay. Shh!" I pat him all over to double-check.

"Stupid driver! She nearly killed us," Mr. Ron says. "Are you all right?"

"Fine." I brush myself off and scramble to my feet. "It wasn't a woman. It was Mr. Sawyer."

He used to be the custodian at our school. But from the back, all Mr. Ron would have seen was his long, blond hair, which looks like the strands of his favourite weapon, the mop.

"That the Mr. Universe janitor? The bodybuilder? Where does he get off disobeying my directions?" He twirls the stop sign like it's a baton.

"He's not our custodian anymore." I shrug my shoulders. "Didn't get along with Mrs. Watier."

"Really? I saw them at the movie theatre together in the summer. Did you catch his plate number?"

"No, but there can't be that many old Beetles in town. Especially orange ones."

"That's where you're wrong. Wednesday night is Beetle Cruise Night at the mall. VWs from all over will be coming. All colours, too. Yup, yup. I plan to go." Mr. Ron sighs. "I learned how to drive on one."

"I thought you didn't drive," I said.

"I didn't say I learned well. Never got my licence but I still love 'em." He lifts his cap and wipes the sweat from his brow. "I would remember that car if Mr. Sawyer had parked it in the lot."

"I don't remember seeing it, either."

"Well, I'm going to report him for reckless driving."

Mr. Ron always threatens to report bad drivers. He wanted to report Mrs. Watier when she cut in front of him on her first day, top down on her TZX. But I don't think he did.

"You sure you're okay?"

I nod.

"And the crazy dogs, they're fine, too?"

"Yup, yup," I answer, the way he usually does. Both dogs strain at the leash, anxious to get going again. The bright green of the park beckons. "See you, Mr. Ron!" I wave as we head onto the field.

We pass by the parking lot of the school and it's almost entirely empty. The teachers sure cleared out of there quickly, but I'm going to try not to over-think this. There's only Mrs. Watier's TZX and a black SUV with a long, white trailer attached. I've never seen it before — it's not like anyone's allowed camping over on school property. What's in the trailer, I wonder. Why is it even in our parking lot?

The dogs won't hold still long enough for me to check it out more closely.

They pull me past the playground swing set and climber. Ping tries to detour through the huge sandbox, but I rein him back, steer both dogs across the soccer field, past the baseball diamond, up the hill and down. Brant Hills Park has so much run-around room for the dogs. Behind the community centre and library, at the far end, there's even a tennis court and a concrete skateboard pod.

The dogs race toward the row of trees that marks the top of the last hill, double sprinkling on most of the trunks. Ping suddenly becomes hysterical, leaping up on one of them.

"What is it, boy? Squirrel?" I scan all the branches. Nothing moving. Oh, wait, what's that? A little knotted black bag sits on the lowest bough. "You need your eyes checked, Ping." I draw closer, reach up, and grab the bag. Oh, man. I can't believe some people.

Dad always says that because we're professional dog walkers, we have to show model behaviour, which means cleaning up after less responsible dog owners, the worst part of the job as far as I'm concerned. But why would anyone scoop after their pet and then perch the bag of poop in a tree? I shake my head and we continue, little black bag jiggling in my hand as the dogs drag me forward.

Over near the library a flash of red under the sun signals that Renée is heading in our direction, a stack of books in her arms. She's studying to be a genius, as usual.

"Hi, Stephen!" She waves.

At least she doesn't call me Green Lantern. Still, I pretend not to hear or see her as I focus on getting rid of the poop bag. Last thing I need is the class hand-waver hanging around. Mom says I need to make a new friend, not to replace Jessie — we can still get together with her discount flight tickets, if I can get over my fear of flying — but just so I have someone nearby. With Princess Einstein on my tail, that will be even harder.

Two tall, domed bins stand at the edge of the parking lot, and that's where the dogs and I head. Because the garbage cans had been knocked over and dumped so often by raccoons or teenagers, the city replaced them with these. They're cemented to the ground, and the chute at the top has a lever to fool the animals, and some people, too. With Ping and Pong yanking me around, I juggle to push the smelly bag through the hole in the dome.

"Why did you put dog doo into the recycling bin?"

"You're following me." I turn to face Renée.

"The path leads this way."

She's right, of course, about the path as well as me dumping the bag into the wrong container. I pushed the bag into the blue bin. The black one is for trash. "I made a mistake, all right?" Number three for today.

"You've probably spoiled all the recycling."

I frown and think about fishing through the bin for that bag, but it's too tall, and I can't see through the chute to find it. "Not the worst mistake I've made today."

"You never know," she says with a shrug. "I mean, how a mistake will turn out. Need help with the dogs?"

How can this recycling-bin error turn out well? I wonder. "No thanks, dog walking is my job. I'm responsible for these guys. And they don't like just anyone."

Meanwhile, Ping wags his whole butt at Renée. His tail propels him into a flip so that he lands on his back, close to her feet, angling for a belly rub. And still he wags.

"This one likes me fine." Renée crouches down to pat him. "Wow, he's fuzzy."

Pong brushes against her for attention, too, whipping his long tail. She reaches to stroke his back, double-handed patting now. "This one's smooth." She squints at me through her glittery glasses. "Why would anyone choose such different dogs?"

"Because … well, the Bennetts rescued Pong from Florida. He's a retired race hound and came with the name Pong. Then, when Mrs. Bennett started her new job with the airlines, she adopted Ping from the shelter to keep him company."

"What a coincidence! She found a dog with a name that matched the greyhound's."

"Of course not. She just named him Ping to be cute."

At that moment Ping snaps at Pong.

"Do they even like each other?"

"Not much." I shrug. "They're still adjusting."

"Let me take the little guy." Renée grabs his leash.

"No." I grab it back. "He's the hardest one to control."

Ping rolls over and sits up, head cocked like he's ready to listen. Renée holds out her hand and he places his paw in it. A perfect shake and perfect dog behaviour, all for Renée. Maybe little dogs like smaller people.

"Okay, fine." I hand the leash back.

A flock of gulls squats down by the football field. When one gull lifts off and flies over us, Ping's calm ends. He leaps into the air, barking. *Rouf, rouf, rowf!*

"Can we let them chase the birds?" Renée asks.

"Absolutely not." I point out a sign that shows a stick man holding a leash attached to what looks like an elephant. "All dogs must be on leashes."

"That's a dog? Looks like a pterodactyl to me." Renée drops Ping's leash. "Whoops, my bad!" She winks at me as Ping tears after the gulls.

I shake my head at her.

"What? Technically, he's still on a leash. Let Pong go, too. C'mon, it's only fair."

Ping's legs turn into wings, his ears, happy flags in the wind. Such joy. I shouldn't do it. I know I shouldn't. Still, I release Pong's leash, too. He sails after Ping, legs stretched full out, long snout open in a big toothy grin.

The gulls leap into the air, screaming insults at the dogs. Pong circles the field after one of them; Ping circles after another. Too late, I spot the skateboarder rolling down the path. Both dogs abruptly halt their bird chase and switch their attention to the wheels rattling over the pavement. They break into a gallop after them.

DAY ONE, MISTAKE FOUR

Letting the dogs run free tops all the mistakes I've made today. Mistake number four, if I'm counting, but it only happened because I listened to Princess Einstein. Ping leads the charge, baring his teeth, growling himself into a froth — a fuzzy streak aimed at those rattling wheels. Pong makes his quiet stealth-lope after Ping, toward the guy on the board.

He's carrying a binder and is dressed in a white shirt hanging untucked over grey dress pants. Not a skateboarder look. Probably came straight from Champlain High School.

"They don't bite!" I call as Renée and I chase after them. "They're really very friendly." Lame words that don't help.

To avoid running over Ping, the guy flips off the board, landing really hard on the black paved path.

"Ping! Pong! Come back here!" Renée calls, as though they will listen to her.

Instead, Ping tackles the skateboarder, licking the guy's face and wagging his behind. Pong stands close, sweeping the air with his tail. If I waited for the dogs to obey me, I'd be waiting a long time. Instead, I run to them and snatch up the leashes, yanking them away from the skateboarder. "Oh, man! I am so sorry!"

The guy doesn't answer for a moment. His knees poke out of his pants, bleeding.

"Are you all right?" Renée asks. "I can run into the community centre and get some ice."

"It's just a scrape," he answers, pushing his bangs out of his eyes. There's something weird about those eyes; they look crossed but they're not. Maybe because one looks more solid, darker. That's it, one's brown and the other is green. Renée's staring and I shove her.

"You're bleeding," she tells him. "They've got a first aid box."

"I'm fine," he repeats. "I'll clean it up at home."

"Why wait? Infection can set in quickly. Have you had a tetanus shot in the last five years?" I ask him.

"Forget about it. I had my tetanus yesterday." He sounds annoyed.

It's at this point that I reach into one of my pockets for a business card. "We're so sorry about the dogs. We should have controlled them better." I hold the card out to him but he's busy scratching behind Ping's ears and smiling. A dog lover, phew! "Listen, your pants are wrecked. Send my dad the bill and Noble Dog Walking will cover it."

"Dogs did me a favour. Tomorrow, I won't have to wear these ugly pants to school." He takes the card anyway. Maybe he knows someone who will need Dad's services.

Pong squeezes in for some pats, now, whipping his tail across the guy's shoulder. The skateboarder reaches way up to stroke his head. "What kind of dog is he?"

"Greyhound," I answer.

"But he's not grey."

"They come in all colours," Renée explains. "Grey means bright or fair in old English."

The guy squints at her

I shrug. "She studies Wikipedia in her spare time. He's a retired racing dog."

"Must've been expensive."

"Oh, probably." Should I have said that? Maybe the guy will think our dog-walking service is only for wealthy dog owners. I pull the dogs away so he can get up. We give him a head start and he skates toward the community centre.

To be extra safe, we double back the other way, heading for the school again. Ping suddenly leaps into the air, barking like crazy.

"What is it, Ping? Another bag of dog poop in a tree?"

"Check out the roof!" Renée points. "There's a dog running around up there!"

DAY ONE, MISTAKE FIVE

"Hey, Mrs. Klein's up there, too." I point to a wiry, short, red-haired lady. Our latest custodian is roaming the roof with the dog and a policeman.

"It's not ball day today, is it?" Renée asks.

Once a year our other custodian used to clear the roof of all the balls that landed there.

"Of course not," I answer. "Would she throw balls down when there're no kids around to catch them?"

"You're right. That would be no fun. She wouldn't need the police for that, either. Maybe the dog is sniffing out a criminal."

The Ping Pong team pulls us past the baseball diamond and goalposts, and up the hills toward the school.

"They're looking for a bomb," Renée says between breaths.

"Oh, yeah?" I bluster, so wanting her to be wrong. "How do you know?"

She points to the white trailer I noticed earlier in the parking lot. "That's where the bomb squad stores its equipment."

She can't possibly know this. "But the trailer's not even marked."

Renée shakes her head. "Imagine the panic if it were. The bomb squad came to my dad's bank last February. That's definitely their trailer."

Of course it is. Princess Einstein knows it all. "We should leave the park, then. Why are we going closer?"

"Because I want to know more."

As we reach the school, Ping wags himself crazy. He rears on his hind legs and bounces on only two paws. Dog body language for *Look at me, pay attention to me. Friends, friends!*

Pong wags, too, and his mouth opens into a grin.

The dog running around the edge of the roof looks like a German Shepherd–retriever cross, gold and black with floppy ears. Sniffing along the edge, he stops to give the Ping Pong team a yip and a wag.

"Would you kindly leave the area," the police officer calls down. "Your dogs are distracting Troy, here."

"Troy distracted them from their walk." Renée may think she's just explaining, but to me, it sounds like she's back-talking the police officer. "Shouldn't he be trained to ignore them?" she asks.

"Yeah, well, no one's perfect. And he's bored."

"Not finding anything?" I ask, trying to smooth things over.

"A bologna sandwich," Mrs. Klein answers. "You kids should eat your lunches."

"Clear out," the cop says more firmly.

Suddenly, Troy forgets our dogs and rushes off barking. He leaps down to a lower level of the roof, nose down, tail wagging, and sniffs at some large pipes. Those pipes lead to the furnace room.

"Let's go," I tell Renée and pull Pong away from the schoolyard.

"Wonder what they found …" Renée says.

I break into a jog now.

"Slow down. What's your hurry?"

"We could blow up!" I answer.

"Nah. We just have to dive to the ground and cover our ears," she says.

"They've gone back inside. Troy must have smelled a bomb in the furnace pipes." My hands get sweaty and I breathe more quickly.

"Or another bologna sandwich. Don't you want to know?" she asks.

"I owe these dogs an hour. A safe hour. We're heading back toward the library."

"Sure, we can check out the school on our way back."

"Hurry!" I run again, giving her no chance to argue. We need to put distance between ourselves and a possible explosion. We breeze by the skateboard park. There are some kids riding their BMX bikes up and down, but no one's in the tennis court. "In here." I take Pong into the court, and she follows with Ping and shuts the gate. There, I throw the ball for them, and we chase them to get it back. Great exercise … for us.

When Renée's phone plays a bar from Beethoven's Fifth, she checks for texts. "It's my brother," she says, as though I've asked. "Attila's in the house now, so I can go home."

"Did you just call your brother Attila, as in Attila the Hun?"

"Yeah, I know, strange name. But my parents are Hungarian. It's popular there."

"Wait a minute, is he the Attila who spray painted graffiti on Champlain High's wall?" Dad read me the story from InsideHalton.com, so I knew all about it.

"How many could there possibly be?" she snaps at me. "He cleaned the wall and finished his community service."

I wince, starting to feel sorry for her now. "Your parents think you can't be alone without *him* there?"

"Um, no," she lowers her voice. "My parents are fine with me being alone in the house. It's me. I don't like to be by myself."

"Bombs don't scare you but you can't be alone?"

"I'm not afraid 'cause I'm with you," she explains. "In the house, when I'm by myself, I hear noises, and instead of thinking, 'Oh, that's just the fridge,' I imagine things. Like it's a burglar or a serial killer moving around."

"I imagine things, too," I admit. "Not so much in my own house, though. Dad's almost always around." I straighten up and puff my chest out. I like that she's anxious about being alone; it makes me feel stronger. And I like that I give her courage.

Out of breath we walk toward the school again. It's still in one piece, so no bombs went off yet.

I see a couple of people near the white trailer. One is wearing a helmet and strange bulky green suit and helmet. The other holds a black box of some kind in his hand. Mrs. Watier's car is gone.

"Oh my gosh, they must have found a real bomb," Renée says.

"Let's head a different way," I suggest.

"Nooooo! I want to take pictures with my phone."

"Does your phone have a zoom lens?" The question becomes pointless as she and Ping tear off. Pong drags me after. Closer and closer to the school we go.

Ping begins barking.

Something is moving, jerking back and forth, actually. It looks like a remote-control transformer, only it's the size of Renée, who is on the short side.

We draw closer. It's a robot with tractor treads. From its outstretched arms, a large, lime-coloured backpack dangles. Wires hang from the bottom.

"What is that thing doing with Reuven's school bag?" Renée asks as she trains her phone in the direction of the robot.

"Shouldn't we be diving down and covering our ears?" I don't ask how she knows whose bag it is.

We watch as the robot zigs and zags its way to the sandpit. Then, it drops Reuven's bag into the sand and backs away. Once the robot returns to the white trailer, there's a loud bang and a burst of sand.

"I don't believe it. They blew it up!" Renée says.

"Did you get a good shot of the explosion?" I lean over her shoulder and she shows me. When

I look up again, I see the guy in the strange outfit — he looks like an astronaut — heading for the sandpit.

When he gets there, he stirs through the sand, putting the bits of Reuven's bag into a bin. Ping barks like crazy at him but Renée drags him away.

We walk toward the white trailer, where the robot now stands, motionless. The police officer pulls out a ramp from the back of the trailer. Then, he uses the black remote to manoeuvre the robot slowly up the ramp.

Ping finds a new reason to bark himself hoarse, which attracts the officer's attention.

"Why are you guys hanging around? This site could be dangerous." His eyes narrow. He looks suspicious.

"We go home this way, sir," I tell him. "Over there's the park exit." I point.

"But we were wondering ..." Renée smiles brightly.

This time the mistake of the day isn't mine. Mistake number five clearly belongs to the Halton Police Department. It's way worse than allowing the dogs to throw the skateboarder down, way more embarrassing than shouting "Fire!" when there wasn't one.

"Why," Renée asks, "did you blow up Reuven Jirad's science project?"

DAY ONE, MISTAKE SIX

Along with her high-pitched tone, Renée tilts her head and squints at the police officer, altogether making it seem like she can't believe anyone could be so stupid as to blow up Reuven's project. Over Ping's barking, Renée continues, explaining to the police officer that Reuven built a mini boom box, how he worked on it for three weeks. I try to quiet the dog down.

The officer shifts on his feet and winces as he defends himself. "Well, the suspect's bag was left unattended on the floor near the computers, right next to the furnace room. A strategic area to affect maximum damage."

Renée often makes me feel dumb, too, like when we work on math or science together: *But why would you do it that way when it's so much simpler to do it this way?* So I nod supportively as I agree with the police officer. "Blowing up the backpack was a sound safety measure."

"Well, Reuven is bit absent-minded," Renée adds, scooping up Ping. Pong stands quietly, leaning against my leg. "But a lot of kids leave their bags in all kinds of places."

I nudge her to try to make her stop.

"Our imaging equipment showed wires." The police officer's voice sounds strained. He's talking through his teeth, which are forced into a grin, maybe to stop him from biting Renée. "And the school received a threat, so we couldn't take the chance."

"We had a bomb threat?" I ask. My mind races. When that fire alarm sounded earlier and we all had to leave without our agendas and homework, Mrs. Watier and Mrs. Worsley must have thought there was a bomb in the school.

"There now, don't go spreading that around."

"No, of course not," I say, wishing I could tell everyone in class tomorrow. It would make up for me panicking over the fire alarm. There *was* a real threat after all.

"Too bad Mrs. Klein is new," Renée says. "Mr. Sawyer, our old custodian, would have recognized Reuven's bag. Still, Mrs. Watier should have known about the science project." ·

Leave it alone, Renée, I think. The officer looks more annoyed with every word from her mouth.

"The principal had to leave, if that's who you mean," he says stiffly, one eyebrow raised and both hands on his hips. "The custodian said something about a wedding dress fitting."

"Mrs. Watier is getting married? But she's already a Mrs.," I say.

"I can't believe women need fittings for their wedding dresses," Renée says. "Why can't they make them the right size in the first place?"

"That's true. Guys only get measured for their tuxes once. Then they pick them up. My dad was a best man last year, so I know." Now Renée has me doing it. "Must be a pain to have to take off for something like that."

"Speaking of taking off," Renée interrupts, "I have to go. My brother is waiting." She puts Ping on the ground again and starts walking with him, expecting me to follow, I guess. No goodbyes or anything to the police officer.

"Me, too!" I tell him. There's nowhere I really have to be. I just want to leave in case he feels the need to arrest one of us for being annoying know-it-alls and I'm the only one left.

The policeman stares after us with both eyebrows up, now.

"Bye." I give him a wave.

Renée and Ping are already way in the lead, so Pong yanks me forward. We leave the police officer frowning and scratching his head.

Pong and I gain on Renée and Ping.

"Want to walk me home?" she asks.

"I've already given the dogs their hour." Really, I'm not happy about the way she talked to the police officer. It reminded me too much of all the times she treated me that way.

"You'll be giving them extra exercise, which will make them behave better. And make you a better dog walker."

She's right about the exercise, but she's being a know-it-all again.

"Please?" Her head tilts again, and her eyebrows and eyes beg along with her tone.

She's lonely. I get that. Since Jessie moved, I never have anyone to walk with, either, except the dogs now.

"Fine."

Her house is around the corner at the end of our street. I always try to keep the dogs off everyone's lawns when we stroll. They gallop along on the stretch of grass between the sidewalk and the street. As we walk east, they're on our left. "Good boy, walk nice," I encourage Pong as we go. "Don't let him pull," I tell Renée.

But Mason Man's big red truck attracts their attention. It's parked across our path, half in and half out of a driveway. Mason Man is large, like his truck, and his arms are as thick as logs. He lives on the other side of the park and owns a golden retriever that we walk. Mason Man does everything with bricks: wishing wells, barbecues, driveways. Today, the sun gleams off his bald head as he spreads mortar on some rust-coloured bricks edging the driveway. It looks like he's building a wall.

"Hi!" I call, but he's concentrating and doesn't answer me.

Renée and I carefully steer the dogs around the back of the truck. Then we turn the corner and

Renée goes into her house. "See you tomorrow," she says.

"See you." Can't avoid her, really; she's in my class, after all. I'm left with the two dogs all by myself now, and I hate to admit it, but Renée really was a big help. As we head back, the dogs become confused and want to stay on my left, just like before. The leashes criss-cross, but I manage to steer Ping off people's lawns. We turn the corner again. This time it's Pong who gives me grief. He pulls ahead to the driveway next to Mason Man's truck. He stretches to reach the pile of bricks, sniffing and saluting the pile with one leg up.

"No, no!" I yell, but it's too late, he lets go a heavy stream.

"Hey!" Mason Man looks up from his wall and shakes his trowel at me. "You know how old these bricks are?"

I want to be honest, but Mason Man's a scary-looking dude on the best of days. With the trowel in his hand, he's armed and dangerous. Still, he's waiting for an answer. "Um, well, they look pretty ancient, actually," I finally answer.

He picks up one from the pile, and I duck away as he shoves it under my face. "A hundred years old."

With a rectangular indent in the middle and the word STANDARD printed inside it, the brick just looks tired to me. You would think the people hiring him to build this wall would spring for new ones.

"These are reclaimed bricks from an old farmhouse on Highway 5. You let that animal pee on antiques."

"Sorry." I try to make it right with him. "If you have a hose, I would gladly wash them down for you."

"Never mind. I don't have time for that."

"Here, Mr. Mason, take my card. If you call me, I'll give Bailey a free walk someday when he needs one."

He holds it in his hand for a moment and shakes his head. "How can I trust you with him if you can't control these two. I should find a different walking service entirely."

"These are new clients for me. We still have to get used to each other," I explain.

"Huh!" Mason Man grunts and stuffs the card in his back pocket. Maybe he'll use the number for Dad to complain later.

Mistake number six of the day becomes ticking off one of Dad's local dog-walking customers, and a meaty, scary-looking one at that.

DAY ONE, MISTAKE SEVEN

What if Mason Man cancels our walking service for Bailey? My first day on the job and I screw up. What will Dad say? I'm going to have to call him right away. But first I rush the dogs back to the Bennetts' house and take them inside, so we can't get in any more trouble. They're panting hard, so I head for the kitchen to fill their water bowls.

Pong puffs hot breaths through my pant legs as he follows close on my heels. Ping snaps up a rubber goose and honks it as he runs around with it lodged in his teeth. *Look at me. Pay attention to me. I have a toy, you don't.* I grab it from him and toss it as far as I can so the noise stops. His toenails scrabble across the hardwood floor as he chases after it. Despite the walk and extra attention, the two still seem desperate for company; it's going to be hard to leave them. Let's face it: back home, I'll be alone, too. Ping shakes the goose at me. "Listen, your mom's going to be home in an hour," I tell them. "I can't stay and play."

Both sets of ears perk up at the word *play*. They haven't really heard anything else. I guess it wouldn't hurt if I hung around and tossed the goose for them for a little while.

At this moment my cellphone rings. Uh-oh! Did Mason Man already complain to Dad? I try to be super professional answering the call. Dad bought me this phone because of his business and insists I answer it a certain way. "Hello, Noble Dog Walking. Stephen here. How can I help you?"

"Hi, Stephen. It's Delilah Bennett. Have you finished with the boys' walkies?"

Ping honks his goose hello.

I stick my finger in my other ear. "Yes, Mrs. Bennett. We're back at your house right now."

"Perfect. As it turns out, I'm going out on another flight. Mr. Bennett won't be home till late."

"You want me to give them their supper?"

Pong lifts one ear up straight and tall at the last word.

"Yes, please. A couple of those little white boxes of sirloin stew for Ping. It's in the cupboard. Half a tin of liver barkies for Pong. His is in the fridge. And Stephen?"

"Yes, Mrs. Bennett?"

"Would it be possible to throw in an extra walk for them? Around seven o'clock?"

"Um, sure." This may make up for losing Dad a customer if Mr. Mason cancels his service. The dogs watch my mouth and face, ears up, tongues out. "An extra walk," I repeat.

The mere mention of the W-word makes them go crazy. Ping wags so hard he flips over. Pong jumps up and places his long toes on my chest. They're super happy and they like me. It's like having two dogs of my own. Closest I ever got to owning any dogs was while playing Minecraft. But I'm going to have to abandon them now, unless I suggest something that's totally against Mom's rules. "Um, Mrs. Bennett, can Ping and Pong hang out at my place?"

"That would be perfect. I'll pick them up from your house later, then."

I hang up and set out the stew and barkies for the dogs, and they race each other to finish. The winner? Ping. He polishes off his own, then muzzles into the greyhound's food and snarfs the rest of that up, too. No wonder Pong is so skinny.

With Dad's delicious dog treats, I manage to get both dogs sitting long enough to snap on their leashes — so much work and we're only a couple of houses away.

As we walk, I know this is definitely a huge mistake to bring the boys home. Mistake number seven. I sigh. We aren't supposed to have any animals in the house because Mom's so allergic. Still, she's on the Paris–Amsterdam–London run and will be away for three more days. I'll keep them outside in the yard the whole time. This should only be for a few hours. For just awhile longer, they won't be lonely.

Luckily, I keep a tight grip on the leashes. I hear the bass pumping before I see it: the orange Beetle driving by at a clip. And what kind of VW makes an engine noise like that? Ping and Pong pull forward to attack, they're so mad. Do they remember our last encounter? As I struggle to keep them back, I notice a different person driving this time. I could swear it's our principal, Mrs. Watier.

My eyes follow the Beetle as it crosses the intersection and doesn't turn. Hmm. That is the street where Mrs. Watier lives. Did she really drive for a wedding dress fitting in that old VW when she has a perfectly good TZX? And how did she even get the Beetle from her arch-enemy Mr. Sawyer?

DAY ONE, MISTAKE EIGHT

Back at home, Ping and Pong shove each other around, snapping and growling to get inside first. As fast as we enter the house, I take them straight to the backyard, where I push them out to the patio.

When they realize I'm not joining them, Ping begins barking and Pong scratches madly at the sliding door.

"You have each other. Now play!" I call to them in frustration. But it's no use. Pong is going to tear up the screen if I don't let him in.

Fine. I slide the door open and take them downstairs to the family room. With a laminate floor and an easy-clean leatherette couch, the dog hair shouldn't be a big deal. I can wipe and sweep it up. There, I turn on the Wii. From the screen, Jessie's avatar grins at me. It feels like at any moment, one of those round knob hands will wave at me.

I click onto my avatar, which has the same brown eyes as I do, plus the shaggy black hair. Compared to Jessie's, mine has a straight-line mouth and eyebrows shaped in high arches, which make it look like it's worrying. Jessie's seems like it's happy and excited, just like Jessie. Having the real Jessie around made me happy, too. We had fun together. I only wish he were here to play bowling with me.

I wonder if Renée likes Wii. Anyhow, I'm not totally alone. I do have the hounds. They scramble alongside of me toward the screen. They bark their cheers when the ball strikes down all the pins. I get about six strikes in a row. If I could do this well in any of the sports at school, I'd have lots of friends.

Then I download a movie called *Dog Hotel* and we all relax — Pong sprawls across the entire couch, his horse-head heavy on my lap; Ping lies on his back on the loveseat, paws in the air, tummy cooling and waiting for stray rubbing.

Suddenly, I hear the door upstairs. Ping flips over, growling. Pong leaps from the couch.

I locked the door behind me, so it can't be a burglar. Dad must be home! Oh, no, mistake number eight: I forgot to call him! He's going to be mad when he sees the dogs here.

He clomps down the steps. Ping and Pong run toward him.

"Hi, Stephen …" The dogs hurl themselves at him, throwing him down on the stairs. *Oooph!* They slurp at his face.

When Dad catches his breath, he says in a tired voice, "You brought them home!" He pats them both at the same time, but Ping still snaps at Pong. Dad shakes his head. "What's this going to do to your mother?"

"They've been outside or down here the whole time. I'll vacuum and Mom won't even suspect."

"It's a mistake to get too attached to the clients."

"Oh, don't worry. They're too badly behaved for that to ever happen. Mrs. Bennett was going to be out the whole night, and I just felt sorry for them." Now is the time to tell him about Mason Man, too.

I follow him up the stairs and so do the dogs.

He frowns when he sees them in the kitchen.

"I'll vacuum the whole house, I promise," I tell him.

"As long as your mother doesn't get sick when she steps through the door. Why don't you make us a salad while I barbecue the chicken," Dad says. He's great with a grill, and with meat and dog food. Vegetables, not so much.

As he forages in the fridge, he tosses me a lettuce and a bag of vegetables. Then, he heads outside, dogs at his feet and a tray of chicken parts in his hands, and I miss my chance to explain about Mason Man.

I hang back to work on the salad. Celery in tiny bits, tomatoes in quarters, bite-sized lettuce leaves — I chop and tear. Then I toss everything with a vinaigrette and head outside to the patio table, salad bowl in my hands.

"So, what's new?" Dad asks as he flips the chicken.

Here's my chance. "Um, um. We met Bailey's owner on our walk."

"Oh, yeah, Mason Man? He's not getting a lot of work these days. I'm not walking Bailey very often."

"Really? He was building a wall for someone."

"Well, that's good. Maybe business is picking up."

"I don't know. He sounded really crabby and he did mention something about not using our service." There, that is the truth. I decide to skip the part about Pong's wetting those antique bricks. I want to keep my job, after all. Maybe Mason Man was just grumbling. Probably, he'll never tell Dad.

"Mason Man often tries to do without our service. Hates the expense, really. He'll bring Bailey with him or rush home at lunch to walk him. In the end, he always comes back."

"You may be right," I say.

"Were the dogs good for you?"

My mouth twists to the side. I find it hard to tell the truth on this one. "No. Renée helped me, though."

"New friend?" he asks hopefully.

"Not really. Just some girl."

"What's wrong with girls? Your mom is my best friend."

"Geez, I'm not marrying Renée, Dad."

"Not yet. But if she helps so well with the dogs…. Just kidding. Anyhow, they'll get better."

"Sure. Just look at them right now. They're fine."

"Got a lot of homework?" Dad tries a different conversation.

"No. We had a fire alarm at the end of the day. Mrs. Worsley told us to not bother bringing our agendas home."

"Wow. Really?" Mrs. Worsley called Dad once about not signing my agenda when there wasn't even any homework, so Dad knows not bothering isn't like her.

"Yeah, so I thought we must be having a three-alarm blaze or something."

"But it turned out to be nothing?"

"Well, the bomb squad came later and blew up Reuven's backpack."

"What?"

I explain to Dad about the dog on the roof and the robot carrying out the backpack, which had wires hanging out the bottom. "Mrs. Watier had left for the day for a wedding dress fitting. And we have a new custodian, so she didn't recognize Reuven's bag. It had his science project in it and it looked like a bomb."

"Why were they even looking for a bomb at the school?"

"I'm not supposed to spread it around …" I lower my voice. "But there was a threat." I start worrying all over again. "Do you suppose there's a real bomb still ticking somewhere in the school?"

DAY ONE, MISTAKE NINE

"No. The bomb squad wouldn't leave if there was even half a chance." Dad knows about bomb threats because of his years at the airport. Still, he avoids mentioning that because I'd worry about Mom. "At my school, there used to be bomb threats all the time. Nothing ever blew up."

"Really?"

"Sure, during exam time. Kids didn't want to study, I guess."

"We aren't writing any exams."

"Some big project due for someone?"

I twist my mouth and raise my eyebrows. "Seems extreme."

"Just a joke, then. Heh heh." He sees me staring at him and stops smiling. "Not a good one, though."

I eat my chicken and salad. Even if his reasoning about the bomb threat doesn't make sense, having Dad around all the time makes me feel better. Up till last year, when he quit air traffic, I hardly ever saw him.

After supper, I snap the dogs' leashes on for their seven o'clock walk.

"Do you want me to come?"

I sigh. It would be great to have his company, but most nights by this time, Dad relaxes in his favourite chair with his knitting in hand and his electric footbath at his feet. He started knitting last year, too, when he also quit smoking. He looks pretty comfy.

"No, that's okay. They're my clients."

We head out. The air has cooled a little and the dogs have calmed down with all the attention they've been getting, but I still keep a tight grip on them.

Somewhere, I've read that you should walk dogs on different routes to stimulate their intelligence. So for that reason, and out of curiosity about the orange Beetle, we cross the main intersection to the posher side of the neighbourhood.

The houses sprawl and have triple garages and artsy sculptures in the front yard. Most have pools with sheds that are mini houses on their own. I sigh again. Before he moved in August, Jessie lived a couple of blocks from here and we played and had sleepovers in their pool house. I miss those sleepovers.

The dogs and I have to stroll along the edge of the street since there are no sidewalks. This could be another mistake of the day, as they will probably do their business on someone's very-well-looked-after lawn.

I don't exactly know where Mrs. Watier lives, just that her house is on this side of Brant Street. I'm starting to doubt my eyes by now, anyway. How could it have been her driving? Sure, she sometimes drives a little fast, but would she have such heavy bass playing?

Around the bend of the street is Jessie's old house. I feel like sneaking in the backyard to peek in the pool house, just for old times' sake. But that's not something I'd ever do. He doesn't live there anymore, so it just wouldn't be the same.

Besides, Ping starts barking at this point and Pong yanks me forward. Ahead is the skateboarding dude again, dressed in baggy jeans and a T-shirt this time. He has a wooden ramp in the middle of the street and he's skating up it. His eyebrows scrunch on his forehead, his teeth clench in a frown, and his face is the colour of a stop sign. He looks like a different guy, more than just determined, maybe even angry.

In the middle of the street, really? If the skateboarder lives in this neighbourhood, he must have a driveway big enough to practise safely. Does he have a death wish or something?

I pull the dogs back hard. Ping hacks like he's choking.

The skateboarder sails over the edge of the ramp for a second. Then *crash*, he clatters down onto his side.

For a full thirty seconds, he doesn't move.

Is he unconscious? I grab the cellphone from my pocket to call an ambulance, but then he's back up, cursing and rubbing his elbow. He approaches the ramp again.

Are you kidding me?

I see a car coming around the corner a little too fast, and I want to flag it to slow down.

Crash! The skateboarder's on the ground again. I wave madly at the car.

Does the driver see me? Does he understand someone's lying in the middle of the street? "Stop, stop!" I call.

Happily, the car slows down, gives a honk, and then drives safely around him.

The dogs and I walk up to the skateboarder, whose cheek is bleeding. "Are you okay?"

"Great," he grumbles.

Ping reaches in with his nose to lick his face. The skateboarder pushes him away. Pong wags his tail and whimpers in sympathy but keeps his distance.

"Do you think it's a good idea to practise jumps in the middle of the street?" The words come out of my mouth before I can stop them, my ninth mistake of the day. I'm in shock, so I babble, sounding a lot like Renée, and it comes across as a mini safety lecture. We all know the answer — even the skateboarder.

His nose wrinkles, and his strange two-coloured eyes look up and burn holes into me. "Mind your own flippin' business."

DAY ONE, MISTAKE TEN

Okay, the skateboarder said something way more harsh than *flippin'*. Ping and Pong bark out their disapproval, but I apologize because I did ask a stupid question. I have to drag the dogs away. As we shuffle off, I notice a flash of orange on the left.

The Beetle sits in a three-car driveway. That's Jessie's old house! He never mentioned who bought it. Is that Mrs. Watier's house now? Her TZX isn't there, but that would only make sense if she drove the Beetle home.

I wonder if the skateboarder lives next door to our principal. Or does he just skateboard in random neighbourhoods, maybe so his parents won't know about his dangerous habits?

We circle around the block and cross over Brant Street again, but instead of going through the park, I walk the team through the townhouse complex instead. Lots of dogs live here, so there's plenty of good sniffing for Ping and Pong. We head toward a jogger decked out in a lime-coloured sweatsuit and matching runners. She's flanked by a large, panting Rottweiler.

As we draw closer, his tail stub winds around like a boat propeller.

"Is he friendly?" I call loudly. She's wearing earbuds.

"Buddy loves meeting other dogs," she answers.

The three dogs get tangled up in each other's leashes immediately, and suddenly, there's a low growl and a snap from the Rottweiler. Pong snaps back and they go at it, snarling and biting at each other with fangs bared. Ping barks hysterically on the side as I unwind the leashes. The Rottweiler suddenly turns and lunges at Ping, who squeaks like a toy.

Did the jogger say Buddy loved *meeting* other dogs or *eating* them, I wonder. Finally, I drag my team away from the Rotti.

"They would have worked it out," the lady says.

Much easier to wait when you own the tougher dog. Still, I smile and hand her a Noble Dog Walking business card just in case Buddy needs some exercise when she's away.

Then I lead the Ping Pong team away.

The moment I get through the door, Dad's cellphone rings. "Noble Dog Walking, Jim Noble speaking, how can I help you?" He pauses. "Hello, Mr. Bennett." He pauses. "You're both going out of town!" He shakes his head as he listens. "All right, it will be up to Stephen. But I have to tell you, we don't usually board." Another pause. "Three days would be a long time for them to be alone, I agree. All right. We'll settle up later." He ends the call and chews his lips. "Airline people."

"What are you going to do?" I say sympathetically. But I know Dad wants to expand his business and sell his homemade dog treats and food. He doesn't want to turn down any of his clients' requests. "Mom's going to be away for three more days also."

"Exactly, so we might be all right."

I smile. Real-life dogs are way better than the square-block Minecraft pets. "We'll have to clean really well."

"Or you can take them home and we can just feed and walk them. The Bennetts would be all right with us looking after them either way."

"That would be cruel. These dogs really are social." Still, keeping them at our house, will that prove another big mistake?

"You have to keep them out of our bedrooms," Dad warns. "We shouldn't have allergens in our sleep area."

"Absolutely! They can sleep in the bathroom. No carpets, easy to wash down."

"Good idea."

So that night, I spread out a sleeping bag across the ceramic tile and give the boys some old stuffed animals and half a bag of dog treats. "Dad, we're almost out of liver bites," I call. "Maybe just enough for tomorrow."

"Fine, I'm making some Wednesday."

Perfect. The dogs cozily crunch on the bites I gave them, and we all settle down for a nice quiet night.

Not.

I'm just dozing off when they start.

Snap, growl, whimper, repeat. I think I can ignore it. I know I can. They'll go to sleep eventually.

But then I can hear Pong hurling himself against the door. *Whomp, whomp, whomp.* It can't hold up against him.

My three night lights help me navigate out of my bedroom to the bathroom, where I open the door. Hard to be annoyed when the dogs are so happy to see me, wagging themselves silly, leaping up on my pajama legs.

"Oh, come on, then." I spread out the sleeping bag across my bedroom floor. Hopefully, the allergens will all be trapped in the bag. They seem to settle down nicely. I fall asleep quickly and deeply.

In the middle of the night, the dogs bark like the hounds of Hades, the mythical multi-headed dogs

Renée presented on at school the other day. I get up. "Whatsa matter?" I can barely talk I'm so groggy. "Do ya need to go for tinkles?"

Pong leaps at the window. My room faces toward Brant Hills. Ping jumps on the bed to be able to look out. So much for allergens. I peer out to see what's upsetting them.

The park lights make it bright enough to see a distinctly shaped little car drive across the school parking lot. That old Beetle keeps turning up everywhere. It stops and I pull the dogs away. Can't be Mrs. Watier this time. Or can it? "Just somebody out driving," I tell the dogs.

My explanation doesn't soothe the team. Pong whimpers. Ping gives a few sharp barks. I'm not convinced, either.

Dad comes into my room, rubbing his eyes. "For Pete's sake, what are they doing in here?"

"They were lonely." I frown and point out the window. "There's a car driving around in the school parking lot."

"Big deal. Probably lots of cars drive there. We just don't know it because nobody wakes us." He scratches his stubble. "Look, if you can't settle them down, we'll have to take them back to their house. We need our sleep."

"They'll be okay, Dad. It's just new to them. Shh, Ping, shh!"

Dad shakes his head and trudges back to his bedroom.

I pick the little one up and dump him onto the bed. Pong jumps up to join him. I'll wash the sheets and vacuum my bed when they leave.

They curl up but still end up taking most of the room. An engine starts up in the distance, and Ping growls low and menacing.

I peek out the window again. The Beetle seems to be jerking back and forth across the lot now. It reminds me of the bomb-detonating robot.

Sighing, I settle myself back down into the space left for me on the bed. It's 12:01 on my cell; technically, it could be called tomorrow already. Another low growl comes, this time from Pong. A chill runs up my spine. What bothers them so much about that car? The last mistake of the day, number ten, turns out to be not investigating more closely.

day two

THE GREAT MISTAKE

MYSTERIES

DAY TWO, MISTAKE ONE

I don't sleep great, squished against the wall by Ping and Pong. Next morning the phone wakes me. Dad calls me downstairs and, standing at the kitchen counter, hands me the receiver. It's Mom and she's at the airport in Amsterdam just finishing her lunch. "Hi, Stephen, how are you?"

I tell her about the fire alarm and remote-control bomb-detonating robot. "Then, in the middle of the night, there was a Volkswagen Beetle driving in the school parking lot."

"The new model or the classic?"

"The classic."

"I love those. You don't see them that often."

"It was the middle of the night, Mom."

"You're reading too much into things again. The fire alarm and the car don't have anything to do with each other. People go for drives. Teenagers like to park and kiss late at night, you know." She sighs. "Listen, I heard a great story from one of the other flight attendants."

"Nothing involving pilot errors, right?"

"No, of course not." Over the thousands of miles between us, I can hear the smile in her voice.

I smile, too.

"Yesterday, at LaGuardia Airport, a mastiff escaped from the cargo hold."

"Don't dogs have to be in cages to fly?" Already, her story makes me uneasy. Where are Ping and Pong? Oh good, I can see them outside the patio door. Dad's let them out. "How could a mastiff escape from a cage?"

"They figure he chewed open his carrier, and when the baggage handlers came to get the luggage, he just burst through the door."

"It's really not safe for animals to travel in cargo, is it?"

"Lots of passengers are allergic, not just me, Stephen. It wouldn't be healthy for us to have them in the cabin."

I twinge with guilt over keeping Ping and Pong at our house overnight. Will they make Mom wheeze?

She continues. "So the escape isn't the worst of it. The dog gallops away from the baggage handlers. And, of course, Flushing Bay borders the runway."

"He doesn't drown, does he?"

"No, no, silly." She chuckles. "But he does jump in and starts swimming as fast as he can to get away from them. Forty-five minutes later, the coast guard finally catches up to him. By this time, the mastiff is so exhausted he's happy to get in the boat."

"That's a great story," I tell her. Where are Ping and Pong, anyway? Next door the Lebels have an in-ground pool, and there's a gap under our fence.

I slide the patio door open but don't call out to the dogs. Mom can't know we're keeping them at our house.

"Listen, I've got to go," Mom says. "They've just finished repairing the engine, so we're ready for boarding."

"Did you have engine trouble?" I step outside and walk toward the gap.

"Gotta go. Love you, Stephen. See you Friday." Click.

"Love you, too, Mom," I whisper to a dead phone. Then I look under the fence. "Ping! Pong!"

It's a warm day for October, and I can feel the hair at the back of my neck getting moist. Suddenly, there's a rattle in the bushes behind me. Ping leaps on my back; Pong noses at my knees. I slump under their attack. "Come on in, guys." I sigh but can't help smiling as they follow me.

Inside, Dad smiles back at me and passes a bowl of oatmeal across the counter.

"They fixed the engine on the plane. Mom had to go," I tell him.

He raises one eyebrow. "You know the mechanics always look over the planes between flights. That's how they keep them safe."

After twenty years of working at airports, Dad would know — I shrug my shoulders and sit down to eat. Ping and Pong look hopeful at my feet.

"What will we feed them?" I ask.

"I'm testing out my special dog stew." He buzzes the food processor. "Leftover chicken from last night, mixed with carrots and oatmeal." He sets down a couple of bowls on the floor.

They rush the bowls. Like I said, Dad's a great cook, for dogs.

"Okay, so you're off to school. I'm off to walk other dogs. These guys —"

"I can take them home and let them out at lunch."

"You'll need a note, then." Dad grabs a sheet of Noble Dog Walking stationery and dashes off a permission note. "I've made it out for the whole week."

"Great." I grab it and stuff it in my backpack.

"Hurry and get dressed now. You'll need to leave earlier to get these guys settled."

The first mistake of the day turns out to be not asking Dad to drop off the dogs because I can't hurry enough. By the time I struggle with them and their leashes and walk them to their house, not only do I feel bad for leaving them, I'm also ten minutes late for school, just enough to need a slip from the office.

As I head for the walkway at the front of the building, I'm surprised to see so many kids still outside. They seem to be heading in the other direction, laughing and chatting along the way like it's the most normal thing. This feels like one of those nightmares where everyone knows something I don't. "Hey, guys?" I want to call. But thinking of the fire alarm yesterday and how stupid I looked when I called out then, I stay quiet and try to figure it out myself. Why isn't everyone settling down in their classrooms, waiting for announcements?

Then I spot the two police cars in the parking lot.

I try the front door and discover it's locked. Something is terribly wrong.

DAY TWO, MISTAKE TWO

"School's closed for today. Go home." The custodian, Mrs. Klein, walks up from behind me, coffee cup in hand.

"Why? It's really nice out so we don't even need the furnace today. Did the pipes burst?"

She shakes her head. "A car drove through the back doors." Mrs. Klein sits down on the steps, sighs, and sips from her cup. "I found it when I came in this morning. Still running."

"Was anybody hurt?" I ask.

She shakes her head. "No one was in the car and no one was in the building. Some bricks are damaged, the doors and frame are wrecked, plus a couple of banks of lockers."

"Was it an accident?" I remember Mr. Ron telling me how he learned to drive. Late at night might be the best time to practise in a school parking lot.

She shakes her head again. "Oh, no, someone drove it into the doors on purpose. And the car ran for a long time. The halls are full of fumes."

Something bothers me about this, something I can't put my finger on. "So, when will school open? When the doors get repaired?"

"No, it won't take that long. When the air clears. We've got huge fans in here blowing. Tomorrow we should be fine."

I shrug my shoulders. "So everyone gets a holiday."

"Not everyone," she grumbles. "It's convenient for Mrs. Watier, though. She's going to have extra time to get ready for her rehearsal tea. And good for the rest of the teachers." Mrs. Klein frowns. "But I'm cleaning up the broken bits of wall and locker in here."

"You're not invited to the tea?" I feel sorry for Mrs. Klein. It's like she's Cinderella.

"Well, I'm not part of the wedding party, so that makes sense. I wish they'd remembered to invite me to the special assembly, though. I had to ask them to let me sign the card." Another sigh. "If you do your job right in this business, most people don't think about you much." She sips and swallows hard. "You have a good day, though, and we'll see you tomorrow."

A mom with a little kindergarten-sized kid at her side walks up now, and Mrs. Klein repeats the news.

I stand there for a moment, mouth hanging open, as I take in the details a second time, all the while remembering last night, the dogs growling, that car …

Mrs. Klein didn't say it was a Volkswagen, but when I shake myself out of it, I cut to the back of the school to get to the path. The yellow crime tape screams out warning and danger to me. I feel a little sick but I have to see anyway. A tow truck starts up just as I pass, and sure enough, it drags out a squashed orange VW Beetle.

I take a deep breath.

Nothing to do about it now. First a bomb threat, then a car smashes into the school. Am I the only one who sees the link? Last night we definitely should have called the police.

At least this means I can go get Ping and Pong and give them a morning walk. Mr. Ron twirls his stop sign as I approach the crosswalk. He's wearing his hat backwards today. Makes him look like a big kid.

"Betcha this is your dream come true, Stephen. A day off in the middle of the week. Yup, yup." Mr. Ron grins, then whistles and holds his stop sign up.

"Kind of scary," I tell him as he struts across the street ahead of me. "What if we'd been in the school when the car crashed?"

"Oh, don't you think it was planned to happen after hours?" He tips his head.

"Smashing into a school…. Why would anyone plan that?"

"Maybe Mrs. Watier will get the new gym for your school now. Did you ever think of that?"

"No, I didn't." I step onto the sidewalk and he follows. "Thanks, Mr. Ron."

"Yup, yup. Have fun on your day off."

"Sure." I head straight for the Bennetts' house. I must have left the dogs not twenty minutes ago, and yet, they act as though they haven't seen me in a month. Ping leaps over Pong to get to me. Pong slaps him away with his tail and jumps on my legs for a pat. Ping yelps and springs straight into the air to plant a lick on my lips. Yuck!

Still, they make me forget everything. I sit down with them on the floor, accepting their happiness and patting them everywhere I can reach. Then I snap their leashes on.

I don't feel like leading them past the school. A different walk is not only good for their minds, it's also good for avoiding explosions and car smashes at schools. I head for the other path into the park, the one that leads us right by the community centre. A few skateboarders are fooling around in the concrete pit right next to it. I watch them until I hear some pounding on the library window.

I look toward it and see Renée. She's wearing her hair in pigtails with sparkling clips today; they sort of look like Ping's ears up at attention. She holds up a finger for me to wait.

Then she tears away from the window.

Here she comes, I think, ready to be a know-it-all about everything.

The door flings open.

"I know all about the Beetle crashing into the school already," I tell her.

She ignores my testy tone. "You have to help me," she cries. "You must have seen something. You have a perfect view of the school from your house."

Is it my imagination or has the whole skateboard crowd stopped to listen?

"Maybe I did," I say much more quietly.

A cyclist whirs by us, hand in the air, brushing all the leaves in the tree. He's the tall freckle-faced kid with rusty hair in grade eight at our school, friendly-looking. Everyone calls him Red. At the library, he dismounts and heads past us to lock up his bike at the rack. He doesn't seem to notice us at all. Still, I wait for him to finish.

Then I make what could be the biggest mistake of the day, mistake number two, when I ask Renée, "How can I help you?"

DAY TWO, MISTAKE THREE

Renée looks around and lowers her voice. "Here, let me take Ping."

I hand her his leash.

Suddenly, we hear someone call, "Hey, Ping!" Red, the cyclist, turns from the library door and walks back toward us. Ping rushes to greet him and gets rewarded with pats, so of course, Pong muscles in for attention.

Renée takes deep breaths. I know she's dying for the guy to leave.

He suddenly squints up at me, his grey eyes sharp with suspicion. "What are you doing with the Bennetts' dogs?"

Immediately, I pull out a Noble business card and hand it to him. "I'm their walker. The Bennetts are away for a few days, so I'm looking after Ping and Pong for them."

He studies the card. "Oh, okay." He tries to pass the card back.

"That's all right. You keep it. Maybe you know someone who needs a pet walked."

Renée rolls her eyes.

The cyclist nods. "Our Pomeranian could use a lot more exercise. She's getting a pot." He tucks the card into his front pocket and heads back for the library.

Renée lets go a gigantic sigh.

"I just want to help my dad grow his business, Renée." We start walking, the dogs sniffing along the grass as we go.

"Yeah, well, you're handing your phone number to people you don't even know."

"It's a business phone. That's what it's for." Still, Renée plants a worry in my head. Maybe this is mistake number three of the day, only it's something I do on other days all the time. "We both know Red from school."

"Never mind that now. Come over here. Sit, Ping! Give them treats so we can talk."

Both of the dogs slump under the tree, and I give them each a liver bite.

"So, what did you see?" Renée asks.

"Well, the dogs came to stay with me last night. And around midnight, they started barking out the window. I got up to see what their fuss was about and saw that Volkswagen Beetle in the parking lot."

"Who was driving it?"

"Remember there's only one light over the parking lot — I couldn't tell."

"Darn. So you can't ID the perp for the police."

"No. Why? Are you planning to join the force?"

"My brother texted me twenty minutes ago. The police officers took him in for questioning."

"Can you blame them? He did spray paint a tank crashing into the wall of Champlain High."

Renée frowns. "And the Beetle belongs to him."

"Attila owns a car?" Ping gives a little growl now, so I dump out two more treats for the dogs.

Renée nods. "My grandfather gave it to him."

"But I saw Mr. Sawyer driving it yesterday afternoon."

"You know Mrs. Watier had him transferred to Champlain High."

I didn't know that, actually. "So, he's custodian there, now. I'm glad he didn't lose his job totally."

Pong stretches out and flips to his back. Rubbing his tummy soothes him and me. *Don't get too attached to the clients*, I hear my father's voice in my head.

"My brother and some of his classmates were working on the Beetle during auto shop. Everyone has access to the keys there. Mr. Sawyer probably borrowed it."

"Mrs. Watier was driving it yesterday evening."

"She's marrying Attila's shop teacher, Mr. Moody."

"So, she borrowed it, too?"

Renée nods. "Someone put something in her car's gas tank. It stalled on the way to the high school, so she borrowed the Beetle to get to her appointment."

"The wedding dress fitting, I remember. How did you find out about the gas tank, though?"

She chews the side of her mouth. "Well, my brother and his friends were laughing about it last night."

"How did they know about it?"

"They didn't do it, if that's what you're getting at."

"Well, they do have a strange sense of humour." I stop patting Pong as he sits up and begins scratching his ear. "And your brother's graffiti on the high school wall was a picture of a crash, after all. You can see how the police might suspect him."

She nods as she scrubs at Ping's head. "I swear it wasn't Attila."

"How can you be so sure?" I ask.

"Because he was souping the car up for Beetle Cruise Night at the mall. He might like painting a picture of a crash on a wall, but he would never have crashed that car."

My phone plays a funny half-note and I grab it to answer. "Hey, I'm getting my first text message ever!" I select the little envelope icon and find a strange sentence from someone named M.Y.O.B.

Keep your mouth shut if you know what's good for you. Otherwise, the dogs will get it.

So, who is this M.Y.O.B.? Mistake number three was definitely handing that particular person my business card.

DAY TWO, MISTAKE FOUR

My breathing speeds up and my heart does a drum roll as the message sinks in. "Oh my gosh, Renée. Someone's threatening me."

"Calm down and let me see." She grabs the phone and stares at the message. "We have to take this to the police."

"Are you kidding?" I look at Ping and Pong and want to hide them somewhere. "M.Y.O.B. will hurt the dogs."

"But it will prove my brother isn't the criminal. He doesn't even know your number."

"I may have given him my business card."

Renée nods her head. "Of course you did. Is there anyone in all of Brant Hills who doesn't have the Noble Dog Walking business card with your cell number on it?"

I frown. Dad and I handed out flyers with the card stapled to it. Everyone in the neighbourhood should have one by now. "Pass me back my phone." I grab it, hit reply, and thumb type: *I don't know anything*.

A few moments later, there's a half-chime. Another message from M.Y.O.B. *Fine, better keep it that way!*

"Are you going to the police with me?" Renée asks.

"They're only questioning your brother. They'll find out about all the others who drove the car, without me having to risk the dogs."

"The others were adults. They're going to pin it on a kid first." She frowns. "Are you sure you didn't see something? M.Y.O.B. seems to think you did."

"I wish I could remember. But something bothers me about what Mrs. Klein told me."

"What?" Renée asks.

"She said the halls were full of fumes because the car ran all night. Once the driver jumped out, wouldn't the car just shut down?"

"You didn't hear about the brick on the accelerator?"

"No. You know more about this than I do. Why isn't M.Y.O.B. threatening you?"

"When you were standing at your window, did you have your lights on?"

I think for a moment. "Sort of. Three night lights, anyway."

"Whoever drove that car must have seen you and thinks you saw him."

"You could be right. We need to test that." I think for a moment. "What makes you think it's a him. It could have been Mrs. Watier."

"Seriously, why would she do that to her own school?"

"Maybe 'cause she wants to add a new gym." I repeat Mr. Ron's idea. "With that area wrecked anyway, the school board might let her."

"And the bomb threat? Did she send that to her own office? She's trying to get ready for her wedding this Saturday." Renée pats Ping's back absent-mindedly, without noticing what he's doing, which is licking his personal parts.

"Does your brother like dogs?" I ask.

She glances down at Ping, and he jumps up to lick her face. She pulls away in the nick of time. "No, Attila got bitten once. Badly. But he's still at the police station, remember?"

Beethoven's Fifth suddenly plays from her pocket and she pulls out her phone. She squints at the screen. "Check that. Attila is at home now. Mom's there, too. Gotta go." She stands and Ping and Pong both spring up.

"See, he's been released." I smile. "And we've kept the dogs out of danger." Ping and Pong cool the air with their wagging tails.

"Don't you ever watch crime shows? It's always a mistake to give in to the criminals."

I frown. Renée's almost always right. Mistake number four could very well be doing what M.Y.O.B. tells me.

DAY TWO, MISTAKE FIVE

I feel bad about not helping Renée's brother, so the dogs and I walk her home. On the way we pass Mr. Ron at the bus stop. I barely recognize him without his yellow and orange vest and crossing guard cap. Plus, he has a Blue Jays cap pulled backwards on his head.

"Hi, kids."

I blink a couple of times. He seems happy, and way less sweaty, but his hands look large and empty. "Going to the mall to get a birthday present for my maw." He holds those big hands open to me. No stop sign in them. "Great to have the free day. Yup, yup. Won't be so crowded to shop."

Imagine a guy that age having a "maw" to birthday shop for. What else don't I know about him?

"Whatcha getting her?" Renée asks.

Nosy, although I kind of wanted to know, too.

"I already bought her an ashtray. Sick of cleaning up her butts in the backyard. Had the perfect one, too. But I lost it. Smoking is bad. I shouldn't encourage her."

"See you tomorrow, Mr. Ron."

"Yup, yup." He waves and smiles.

"Geez, how old would his mother be?" Renée whispers to me. "Does it matter if she smokes?"

"'Course it matters. You can't taste your food as well. Your hair and clothes smell. You get yellow fingers and teeth. Blech!" For such a smarty-pants, she could be pretty dumb sometimes.

"But she's probably a hundred and fifty. Don't all old ladies have yellow toenails and smell gross?"

"Not my grandma." I give Renée a hard stare. "She paints her nails and wears lemon perfume."

As we near Renée's corner, we see Mason Man standing back with a grin on his face, admiring the brick wall he put up along the driveway. I have to tug to keep Pong from saluting it.

"Hi, Mr. Mason, looking good." I'm hoping my flattery will help him forget about the dog-peeing incident.

"Yeah, you got that right. The whole house will fall down before this baby will budge."

Renée struggles to keep Ping on the other side of the walk. Mr. Mason's work should be safe. "But they're used bricks, aren't they?" she asks.

I turn and raise my eyebrows at her. "They're antiques!" *The whole house will fall down* … that remark reminds me about the car driving into the school. "Mr. Mason, did anyone steal one of your reclaimed bricks?"

"No, I keep track of every one of these Standards. People like them for bookshelves and candy dishes, so I lock 'em up at night."

"Candy dishes? Really?" Renée says, and I elbow her.

Mr. Mason doesn't seem to notice. "Say, it looks like I'm going to get some work at your school. I'm going to take you up on that free dog walk you offered."

"Great, great!" I lie politely. I've got Ping and Pong for another two days. When will I find the time? "Just give me a call and we'll arrange something."

"I'll call your father. Bailey knows him. Tell him I'm going to need another bag of those liver bites, too. That dog will do anything for those treats."

"Sure will, Mr. Mason."

We turn the corner, dogs leading the way.

"What's with the brick question?" Renée asks when we're far enough away from Mr. Mason. "We don't even know what kind was found on the accelerator."

"Just thought we'd eliminate that possibility." We arrive at her house now and stand in front of it, talking.

"So you *are* helping me clear Attila, after all." She smiles and punches my shoulder.

At the front window, the curtain rustles and her brother steps in front of it, his arms folded. He wears his hair in a mohawk and lifts weights, I'm sure, because his T-shirt looks tight around the top of his arms and chest. Attila stares at Pong, a bullet-hard stare. Then, eyes narrowed, he looks at me.

Mistake number five might be Renée's, because right now, I'm thinking I'll probably find more evidence that will prove Attila guilty instead.

DAY TWO, MISTAKE SIX

As she hands me Ping's leash, Renée doesn't seem to notice Attila scowling at the window. "Aren't you afraid the criminal will find out you're investigating?"

"Sure," I answer. "But we have to find out who it is. Or I'll never feel safe."

Her smile stretches into a grin. "You always see way more into things than other people do. With you on the case, we're bound to find the real criminal."

Mom and Dad always say I see more into things, too, only they make it sound like a bad thing. I grin back at Renée. She's right about everything, after all. "Thanks." I spot Buddy the Rottweiler coming from the end of the block. "Gotta go now. Pong doesn't like that dog heading our way." I start walking the other way, pulling the dogs along.

"Try to think about what you saw that night!" she calls after us.

If I can hear her, then Buddy's owner, the lady in the lime running suit, can, too. And who knows who else is listening.

I turn and, leashes still in my hand, put a finger to my mouth. "Shhh!"

A bicycle whirs by and Ping catches me off guard as he lunges at it. *Rouw, rouw, rouw!* Red, the kid from grade eight, just smiles and calls to the dogs as he continues home. I pull Ping back while keeping Pong tight against me.

Had Red heard her? Too late now.

The dogs wag goodbye to the friendly voice, and we continue past the Bennetts' and our house. It hasn't been a full hour's walk, so for old times' sake, we cross Brant Street over to Jessie's side of the neighbourhood. No sign of the skateboarding kid, but his school didn't get closed for the day, so he's probably still in class. We walk around the bend and Ping begins yapping.

There's Jessie's old house. Mrs. Watier's TZX isn't sitting in the driveway, which is a good thing because all the shrubs, the light posts, the door-frame, and the mailbox are wrapped in toilet paper. An autumn breeze blows through some of the strands, which annoys Ping and now Pong, who strains to attack.

I yank the leash. "C'mon boys. It's just a joke someone played on the future newlyweds." Doesn't seem funny to me, a waste of paper and a mess to clean up. I glance back. Well, maybe it's a little funny. The house looks like it's wearing little wedding veils, which makes me smile. I peek into the backyard and see that our old playhouse looks bridal, too.

We continue on, and at the strip mall, just before we cross over Brant again, I see him getting out of his car heading for the pizza place: Mr. Sawyer, our former custodian. His long, blond hair kind of screams *Look at me*. I remember how poor Mrs. Klein said no one notices you if you do your job right.

But I sure did notice Mr. Sawyer pushing his mop around, until about the second week of school. Renée says he purposely tripped Mrs. Watier with it and sent her flying. I don't think that could be true. There's that rumour about them having gone out, after all. He's just a very strong guy, former Mr. Universe and all, the Superman of mopping. He knocked kids down all the time, especially if they tracked in dirt. Mrs. Watier might just be more tippy with those high-heeled boots.

"Hi, Mr. Sawyer!" I wave to make sure he realizes that someone cares enough about him to remember his name.

A mistake, number six of today, 'cause I'm always counting.

Mr. Sawyer's brow furrows and he frowns. It's clear he doesn't remember me. The dogs start barking — there's something white fluttering from behind him. He gives the Ping Pong team a glare. Not a dog lover. When he finally turns away, I see a long piece of single-ply tissue sticking to the back of his jacket. If he is M.Y.O.B., he might now think I'm investigating him.

DAY TWO, MISTAKE SEVEN

"Toilet papering Mrs. Watier's house — that's a joke, not vandalism," I tell Ping and Pong as they strain to go back. "People tie signs and cans to wedding cars all the time." Mr. Sawyer may have driven that orange Beetle in the afternoon, but the toilet-papering joke doesn't mean he drove it into the school.

Do you joke with someone who had you transferred? Someone who might have broken up with you? She is marrying someone else, after all. But now that he works at Champlain High School with Mrs. Watier's fiancé, maybe the two of them like to play tricks on each other.

As a quick double-check, I pull out my cell and press "return call" on M.Y.O.B.'s text. Then I stop the call immediately. What am I thinking? What if M.Y.O.B. really is Mr. Sawyer? He'll imagine I'm trailing him, and it will be me and the dogs, alone against the Mad Mopper.

I stash the phone in my pocket and walk a few steps. Pong jostles into me from the back. That funny *bleep, bleep* sound comes from my pocket. My classic mistake, number seven of the day, has to be butt-dialing M.Y.O.B.

Luckily, nothing rings, buzzes, or sings on Mr. Sawyer. I grab my phone, press "end," and lock the keyboard this time. Meanwhile, Mr. Sawyer disappears into the pizza place.

That probably puts him in the clear, although he could have left his phone in the car.

The dogs don't give me a lot of time to stew about it. Across the street, a rabbit hops through one of the yards, and they drag me toward it. From there I lead the team to our house rather than the Bennetts'.

"Da-ad!" I call as we step inside. "I'm home! School got cancelled today!"

"I heard. Lucky!" he answers from the kitchen.

As usual, he's acting all positive so I don't get anxious. But this time, it's about a real crash, not just a threat.

I unleash the dogs and they rush to Dad. I follow behind in time to see Pong jump on him and Ping just jump, up and down, like a Jack-Russell-in-the-box.

"Down!" Dad rustles a bag of his liver bite treats, and Ping immediately stops. He shakes Pong off his legs with his knee. "You know, you could work on training these guys while their owners are away."

"I'm trying to get them to walk nicer. Remember you suggested they were too hard to even take out together."

"That's true. You're doing well."

My mouth opens for a moment to say something else. But if I talk to Dad about the threatening text, won't he just tell me I shouldn't worry, that it's just some kid fooling around?

Or worse, he could decide we have to go to the police, which would put the dogs in danger. I decide not to share with him. Instead, I know I need to tell him about the free walk he has to give, but I stall with some good news first. "Mr. Mason wants another bag of treats for Bailey."

"That's great. He told me they were way over-priced. He can be a real tightwad sometimes."

I cringe as I get ready to deliver the not-so-good news.

"I'll take the liver out of the freezer right now so I don't forget." He opens the door and removes a small bag. "I'll buy some more, too. It's on special this week."

I clear my throat. "I may have offered Mr. Mason a free walk for Bailey."

Dad drops the bag on the counter and stares at me. "We already have his business. Why would you do that?"

"Well, I am working on getting Ping and Pong to walk only on city property but sometimes they get confused …" I explain to Dad about the peeing incident.

"Oh, that big cheapskate. He was just trying to get something for nothing. Dogs always mark their territory on whatever's left around: construction material, workers' tools, even lunch pails if they're within reach. He knows that. He has a dog."

"Dad, I'm sorry. I offered to walk Bailey to make up for it. But he insists it has to be you."

"You have these guys to look after. And they're not well behaved enough to just add a third dog."

"Yes. So you can keep the money from one of the extra walks I've given them."

Dad reacts immediately. He's a bit of cheapskate himself. "That's a great solution. You're a very smart kid!"

DAY TWO, MISTAKE EIGHT

If I'm such a smart kid, why can't I figure out who smashed the Beetle into the school? After all, it's someone who thinks I know. "Dad, is it okay if I use the computer for a while? I want to do some research."

"Go ahead. I need to walk five Yorkies. New client of mine."

"Five, Dad? All with one owner?"

He nods. "And they have little-dog syndrome. They're yappy and snappy ..." He holds up a bag of his special treats. "But I have my secret weapon."

Immediately, Ping and Pong sit dutifully at his feet, watching that bag. Dad flips them each a liver bite.

"Have a good walk," I tell him and head for the computer.

The dogs follow me to the den and slump down at the chair in front of the screen. Feeling their warm breath on my ankles, I Google "reverse phone number lookup."

I select Canada411.ca and copy M.Y.O.B.'s number into the search bar. After a moment a message reads: *No listings were found. Please try again.*

Of course. It's a cellphone. You can't look up names and addresses for those. Or can you? I immediately Google that question and read an article about how the police have to get court orders before phone companies will release information on unlisted numbers.

Ping barks a warning as my phone rings.

Not M.Y.O.B. I sigh with relief. *R. Kobai*, the caller name reads. Kobai is Renée's last name. Still, I answer in official Noble Dog Walkers' form.

Renée doesn't even say hello. "The police are charging my brother now."

"Really? When so many other people drove that Beetle?"

"Yes, well, they traced the bomb threat email to an IP address at Champlain High."

"Don't tell me. It's the computer that your brother usually works on in IT class."

"Yes, but you know everybody uses each other's computers sometimes."

"Sure."

"You need to bring your cellphone to the police now and show them the threat."

"I don't think that's a good idea," I tell her.

"Why not? The police will find the guy immediately and the dogs will be safe."

"That's what you think. Have you never seen the spy shows where they give an agent a phone to use and then throw it away?"

"Yes, but secret agents have tons of money for all kinds of gadgets. Our criminal probably doesn't."

"Maybe, but I think they may be watching me. If they see me going to the police, they're going to pitch their phone, which will be registered to a phony name, anyway. Then they're going to come for Pong and Ping."

Renée sighs at the other end.

"We are going to go to the police, eventually. I just want to have more information for them to go on."

"That's dangerous, too, and you know it. The criminal may notice."

"I know. Listen, do me one favour. Dial this number from your own phone and see if a cell rings in your brother's room."

"He didn't do it. I already told you."

"We're eliminating suspects. Humour me." I give her the number.

"What if the real criminal picks up?"

"Just say 'Sorry, wrong number,' and hang up quickly. At least they won't link the call to Noble Dog Walking."

"Okay. Hang on." I can hear the *blip, blip, blip* of her cellphone dialing, then the drum roll of a phone ringing and ringing. "How long should I give it?"

"I don't know. Are you near his bedroom? Can you hear anything going off?"

"No. And I'll tell you why not. It's not Attila. If it were him and he was threatening you, he'd block his number."

"He can do that?"

"Star sixty-seven on his phone. M.Y.O.B. has to be pretty stupid not to use it, too."

"Um, *I* didn't know that."

"No, but you wouldn't prank call someone. Or threaten them, either. If you did, you would find how to do it anonymously beforehand."

"You're right." I sigh. "So we know our criminal has to be pretty stupid."

"Cross Attila from your list. He's not stupid."

"Okay. Bye."

Once she's gone, I decide to look up Mr. Sawyer in the online phone directory. There are quite a few in the Halton region, but there's an R. Sawyer who lives right on Jesse's old street. The teachers used to call Mr. Sawyer Bob, which is short for Robert. Has to be him! Mr. Sawyer is Mrs. Watier's neighbour, and she practically fired him! Wow. I'd be pretty annoyed with her if I were him. 'Course, he did mop her down, whether accidentally or not.

Did he not have his cellphone with him when I called M.Y.O.B.? Had he thrown it away already?

Then a bigger question hits me. If you've already driven a car into the principal's school, would you bother TP-ing her house as well? It seemed like overkill.

I can't think of anything else to look up, so I close the browser. The dogs follow me back upstairs to my bedroom, where I gaze at the school from my window and try to imagine that Volkswagen all over again, try to remember something that I may have seen but just didn't register. Maybe I should have someone hypnotize me, like they do on crime shows.

Over on the far corner of the field, just past the school, I see the bus pull up and Mr. Ron get off with a large pink bag in his hand. He's been my crossing guard since kindergarten, and I realize I still don't even know where he lives. I look to the left of our house: a retired couple lives there. And to the right, the Lebels, a family with two little white-haired kids, are our neighbours. Beyond those houses, we don't really know anybody on our street, except for the Bennetts and only because they work for the same airline as my mom and use our dog-walking service. Anyone in our neighbourhood could have seen what happened last night in the park. Had the police checked with them?

I come up with a plan and call Renée back. "Do you want to go for a walk tonight? I mean really late?"

"Sure. What time should we meet?"

If I were watching some mystery movie right now and the twelve-year-old kids decided to wait till their parents were asleep to sneak out in the middle of the night, I'd know it was a mistake. That something awful would happen. Mistake number eight today is not listening to that voice inside that tells me the very same thing.

"Midnight at the front of the school."

DAY TWO, MISTAKE NINE

"Walk nice!" I command Ping as I hold a liver bite close to my knee. I'm taking him around the block on his own so I can concentrate on training him properly, hoping a one-on-one session will help for our midnight walk. When he follows right at my heel the whole way, I give him one of Dad's magic treats.

It's at this point my cellphone rings.

"Noble Dog Walking, Stephen Noble speaking."

"I've got a brilliant idea."

"Hi, Renée. What is it?"

"Ask your dad if I can come for a sleepover."

"It's the middle of a school week and you're a girl. He'll never go for it."

"Don't tell him I'm a girl."

"He already knows."

Renée's voice goes up a notch. "Maybe he'll forget. Just say you're worried about Renée." She sounds desperate. "With all the fighting going on at my house, it's not a good environment for a kid to be in. Your dad's not going to say no to that."

For her to plead for this sleepover, I have to think she's not having a great time. "Um … just how bad is it over there?"

"Terrible. My father wants to send Attila to military school. Mom believes he's innocent.

They're all yelling at each other. And all the while, they tell me to go to my room. That this doesn't concern me."

"Okay. I'll do my best. Call you back later."

As I glance down to slip my phone back into my pocket, the leash pulls hard. A skateboard rattles in the distance and I look up.

It's that guy we knocked down in the park, the one who seemed so angry the other day. Ping lunges for him but I snap him back. "Pssht! No! Leave it!"

Ping looks up at me and argues. *Rouf, rouf, rouf!*

"No, no!" I hold one finger up with another liver bite tucked in my hand. "Sit!"

He whines as he lowers his butt. His mouth opens and his tongue quivers as he pants.

"Qui-*et*!" I warn.

He licks his chops and shuts his mouth. His eyes laser on to that liver bite.

"Good boy." I finally give it to him.

"Where's the other dog?" The skateboarder walks back toward us, his board tucked under his arm. His brown eye studies me; his green one seems to watch Ping.

I hesitate for a moment. Last time we met this guy, he was swearing at me.

"You know, the greyhound — where is he?" He's smiling and friendly today.

Why was he in such a bad mood the other evening?

"Oh, Pong is at home right now. I'm giving them individual attention."

"Good, 'cause, you know, I thought maybe something had happened to him."

"No. Nothing." His suggestion makes me nervous. Does this skater boy know who's threatening us? "We look after our customers well. The dogs are either on a leash or in a fenced area at all times."

"Glad to hear that."

"We have surveillance cameras on the property and we lock the gate," I bluff. I watch the skater's face.

He doesn't react.

This is easily mistake number nine today. Skater dude can check our house. He can lift the latch on the gate; he can look for cameras.

For now, he smiles and gives a finger wave as he steps on his skateboard again. "They should definitely be safe, all right. See you around."

DAY TWO, MISTAKE TEN

I take Ping back in the house and don't bother with Pong. He's quieter and better behaved, anyway.

Dad comes back from walking the Yorkies and joins us in the kitchen, where I set down water bowls for the dogs. "Dad, have you ever thought of putting cameras up or locks on the gate?"

Dad just stares at me for a moment like he's trying to read inside my brain.

Lap, lap, lap. The dogs drink. There's nothing quite as calming as the sound of their tongues slurping up the water.

I smile. "Wouldn't surveillance be a great way to keep the burglars and kidnappers away?"

He blinks and shakes his head. "No, that would make me a paranoid person." He turns and washes his hands at the kitchen sink, shakes the water off his fingers, and glances back at me. "Which I'm not." He grabs a package of tortillas from the cupboard and rips them open with his teeth. "Sit and have lunch with me."

I pull out a chair and watch as he sprinkles cheese on the tortillas, drains a tin of tuna, dumps it on top, and slides the plate in the microwave. "Are you thinking of branching out into cat food?" I ask.

"Never, but a little bit of kale or spinach would make this a complete meal for a dog."

"We could probably use the vegetables, too."

Dad takes a bag of mini carrots from the fridge, rinses them, and puts them on a plate with a white salad dressing as dip. "Satisfied now?"

I nod and throw the Ping Pong team a carrot each. When Dad serves up the fishy pizza, I let the dogs sample first. They don't seem to mind that there's no kale on it. Then I taste. Not bad. A splash of salad dressing improves the flavour.

"You know they have surveillance cameras at the school," Dad says as he finishes his tuna-cheesy thing.

"Really?" I continue eating mine till I'm done. Then I lick the fish from my fingers.

"Says so right here on InsideHalton.com. You can read the article." He passes me his iPad with the page open on the screen.

Ping yips at me, so I set out some plates of Dad's homemade dog food. That gives me peace and quiet to scan the article. Nothing new, a bit about the bomb squad blowing up a school bag, a longer bit about the orange Beetle crashing into the school and how a red brick on the accelerator kept it running all night.

"It says the images were too grainy to identify a driver."

Dad nods his head. "Maybe the guy was too far away. Remember, it's the brick on the accelerator that sent the car through the school."

The brick, the *red* brick — the colour is a new detail! The reclaimed Standards that Mason Man used were red. He might be the only person I didn't see driving the VW that day, but he certainly needed the work the crash provided him. He had the motive.

Pong runs his long nails on the patio door, letting me know he wants to go out. I delay for a moment because I need to be with the dogs so they don't duck under the fence to visit the Lebels' pool and so M.Y.O.B. doesn't do anything to him.

"Dad, would you happen to know Mr. Mason's cell number?"

"Why? Maybe you should let the dog out."

"In a minute. I just want to compare his number with another caller's on my cell."

Dad reads out Mr. Mason's phone number but it doesn't match M.Y.O.B.'s.

"Okay. By the way, I didn't tell you that my friend Renée —"

Pong whimpers. Ping barks. Heads tilted, eyes riveted on me, they demand I pay attention.

Dad interrupts, too. "You've finally made a friend. That's good."

He's forgotten I mentioned her before. Is she a friend, really? I wonder. Or just another lonely kid like me? She likes how I read a lot into things and she's smart, even if she can be a know-it-all. "Yes, well, Renée's having a hard time of it at home. Attila, the brother, is charged with the car crash into the school and I'm worried ..." I touch the patio door handle to get the dogs to stop their noise. I grab a treat for them, too, and let them see it. Instantly, they sit, quietly studying my hand.

"His brother is the one who drove that Beetle?" Dad asks.

I don't correct him on the "his" part. I have to work up to that. "The Beetle belongs to Attila, yes. And he drives it, but Renée doesn't think he's the one who wrecked the school with it. Anyhow, Mr. and Mrs. Kobai are arguing and Renée asked to sleep over tonight."

"Your mother's not here and all. Better have them call me."

"So it's a yes, if it's okay with them? We won't stay up late. Renée's a keener about school and homework …"

"I like him already. Absolutely. He'll get a break and you'll have a distraction from the car crash, too."

Renée was right again. Still, what will Dad say when he sees she's a girl? He'll be okay with it, I think. I mean, he can't say no once her parents call. I slip the dogs their treats and open the door, and they push each other to get out first. I follow. "Thanks, Dad." Mistake number ten of the day belongs to him if he thinks having Renée over will stop me thinking about that Beetle. My investigation has only begun.

🐾🐾

On the seven o'clock walk that evening, I swing the dogs around a different way to pick up Renée. We walk by Mr. Mason's house. It's a small brick bungalow with a red-brick drive and walkway. The flowerbeds are also edged in red and there's a brick patio in the front.

Mr. Ron and Mr. Mason sit there chatting, frosty glass mugs in their hands, Bailey sprawled at their feet. The old golden retriever gives us a slow wag and then hoists himself to his feet to greet Ping and Pong.

"Hey there, Stephen," Mr. Ron calls, lifting his mug in a salute.

"Hi, Mr. Ron." Big hands, round belly, shaggy hair, he's like a teddy bear compared to strong, bald Mason Man. Opposites, like Ping and Pong. Or maybe even me and Renée. How is it that I've never seen them together before?

The dogs all seem happy to see each other, but I keep a tight rein on my team so as not to allow the leashes to tangle the way they did when they met Buddy, the Rottweiler.

"Hi, Mr. Mason," I call and he just grunts at us. The bricks around his house are a different red than the Standards he used at the house near Renée's. There might be a million different kinds of brick that could have been used on that Beetle's accelerator. No clue here.

We continue on to Renée's house. Ping does walk closer to my heels, looking up constantly to my hand, but my treat bag is almost empty. One of my arms has definitely grown longer with Pong's constant pulling. I ring the doorbell and my heart stops when Attila comes to the door instead of Renée.

"I — I —" I stutter. Ping growls low, which starts Pong on a rumble, too.

"Renée told you I was charged, didn't she?" He scowls at me, and then turns to face her. "What a big mouth."

Renée moves around him with a small kiwi-coloured rolling suitcase. Her hair is pulled back into a ponytail, one bright-red stone sparkling from the elastic. "Stephen is helping me find the real crook."

Attila just grunts and shuts the door after her.

The dogs instantly change into a super happy mood. Ping gives a nibble at one of the suitcase wheels.

"Leave it!" I tell him and lure him off it with a liver bite.

Renée pats him, and I pass her the leash so we can roll along.

"Why isn't Attila in jail?" I ask her.

"Too young. He's out on bail."

"You shouldn't have told him about me helping you!"

"Look, Attila does crazy stuff, no question about it. He might even prank call girls he likes. But he blocks the number. And nothing rang in his room when I dialed M.Y.O.B.'s number like you asked me. Doesn't that prove he's innocent?"

"No. Ringing could have helped prove him guilty. That's all. Let's drop off your suitcase at my house and keep walking, so these guys get their exercise."

We pass by the wall Mr. Mason finished earlier and make sure to keep the dogs away from it, which reminds me, "Did you know the brick on the Beetle's accelerator was red?"

"No, I didn't."

Score one for me over Princess Einstein. I nod. "I read about it on InsideHalton.com."

"These are red." She points. "Or do you consider that colour brown?"

"Maybe rust, I don't know. But so are all of the ones he used in his own landscaping. There must be tons of red bricks around."

"Um, Stephen, just to let you know, my brother has a bookshelf made of planks and bricks."

"Red ones?"

"Uh-huh."

"Did you check if any are missing?"

"No." She sighs. "But if it makes you happy, I will."

"We have to treat everyone as though they're a suspect."

"Sure we do." She rolls her eyes at me.

"At the very least, we can stay a step ahead of the police about Attila."

"True." She brightens over that answer. "Ping's walking a lot better now."

"That may end when I run out of these." I rattle the treat bag and pull back on Pong to try to get him to heel nicely, too. When he slows, I slip him a treat and Ping yaps his complaint to me.

"What happens when the dogs go back to their owners, Stephen? Will you tell the Bennetts about the threat?"

"No. If I tell any adults, the police will become involved immediately. You know that. I just hope this will all be over by then." We turn onto the walk-way to my house, and I open the door for Renée, who pushes her suitcase into the house. Dad's not around to meet her. Probably a good thing.

On the rest of our walk, I show Renée Mrs. Watier's house, complete with its toilet paper wedding veils. "Do you think someone is trying to sabotage her special day? First, there's a bomb scare on the day of her dress fitting. Then someone puts something in her gas tank. A car crashes into the school in time for her rehearsal tea."

"That's brilliant reasoning, Stephen!" Renée says. "What do you have in mind for tonight's midnight walk?"

Later, when Dad meets Renée, his eyebrows raise. "Stephen, you never told me Renée was a girl."

"You knew that," I answer. "Remember when I told you she helped with the dogs? You even said I should marry her."

"Slipped my mind."

"Do you not think boys and girls can be friends? Lots of people are like that," Renée says to him.

"No. That's not it. I haven't spoken to your parents yet, and I need to know they're all right with you staying over at a boy's house. Especially when his mom's not here. Would you like to get them for me?" Dad hands her the phone.

She dials. "Hi, Mom. I'm at Stephen's. Yes, I want to have a sleepover at a boy's house." She pauses. "You don't think boys and girls should have sleepovers? But you and Dad have them all the time." Renée turns to Dad and hands him the phone. "She wants to speak to you."

Dad listens for a while. "Yes, it's all right with me. Stephen mentioned something about doing homework together, and we do have a spare room … Yes, it sounds like you're going through a rough time … I hope things turn out well … Yes, I'll make them both lunches … Thank you. I'm glad Stephen has made a new friend, too."

When he hangs up, he sends me up to the guest bedroom with clean sheets. It's not exactly like a sleepover with Jessie where we pile sleeping bags on the couches in the basement.

But we do end up playing Wii sports. We design a great avatar complete with glasses and a ponytail to represent Renée. I beat Renée at bowling, but she's a whiz at golf and gives me some great pointers.

Before bed, we coordinate our phone alarms and set the volume on low.

"Goodnight," I tell Renée and head for my own room. There I lie down and count Jack Russells and greyhounds jumping over fences till my eyes grow heavy.

day three

THE GREAT MISTAKE

MYSTERIES

DAY THREE, MISTAKE ONE

At midnight, my phone buzzes me awake and I hear the musical notes from the guest room. I dash to meet her in the hall, Ping and Pong crowding around my feet. "We better go quickly before the dogs wake Dad."

"Wait," she whispers. "Put something in your window so we can test out how much the criminal can see from the park.

"Good thinking," I whisper back. We set up a stool in front of my bedroom window and plonk Peanut, my stuffed elephant, on it. Ping leaps up to sink his teeth into the stuffie and pulls him down. "Leave it!" I snap, and when Ping sits nicely, I give him one of the last liver bites. Dad better have more treats ready for tomorrow's lunch-hour walk.

I set Peanut back on the stool. "Shh, shh," I tell the dogs as we quietly head downstairs and out the door.

"Is the light from the moon about the same?" Renée asks.

"Maybe the moon's a sliver bigger." We head quickly for the walkway into the park. The dogs love the brisk pace, and we jog with them to the parking lot of the school. We stop and turn around. "Can you see Peanut?" I ask Renée.

"Perfectly," she answers as we stare up at my bedroom window.

I look and can even make out his glossy black eyes. "So, you're right about the criminal spotting me. I wonder which houses get a good view of the parking lot besides ours."

We look around in the darkness. Over across the field, I see a small, red dot glowing. A cigarette? I point to it, and Renée and I drift silently closer to the chain-link fence along the edge of the park to investigate.

"How much farther can we go and not be spotted?" Renée asks.

"I don't know." The first mistake of a brand-new day (since it's past midnight): we walk close enough for an old lady sitting in her backyard to see us. "What are you kids doing up at this hour? I'm gonna call the police on you."

DAY THREE, MISTAKE TWO

"She's smoking a cigar!" Renée whispers at me.

"Not just any cigar. It's a Habanos," the lady growls. Her cheeks puff out, and a cloud of smoke rises from the end of the fat brown cigar. "I'm not deaf, ya know."

I squint.

"Can't a person enjoy a smoke on her birthday without a bunch of kids hanging around? What are you even doing out of bed?" She's a pale-skinned lady dressed in a flowered muumuu. Her hair is frosty white. In one huge hand, she clutches a cell-phone. Her thumb looks poised to key in a number. "Yup, yup, gonna call the police."

"Sorry," I say. "Please don't. Our dogs needed to go out suddenly. Supper disagreed with them."

She takes a puff and lays the phone down on the little table beside her.

"Are you Mr. Ron's mom?"

She squints at me through the smoke. "How did you know that?"

"He takes me across the street a couple times a day. Has since I was little. I can see a strong family resemblance." Her hands are as big as his, and she gestures and talks in the same way.

I notice a large, red ashtray in her lap. "Did you get that from him?" I ask. "He told us he wanted to buy you one." *To replace the one he'd already lost, hmm.*

"Yup, yup. It's handy, nice and big. Just wish it wasn't breakable. I'm kind of a dropsy sometimes. So is Ron."

"Ma'am, were you sitting outside last night around this time?" Renée asks.

"Yup, yup. That's what I told the police already. But I can't see the parking lot from here. Turn around and look yourself."

I can't help myself. I do as she suggests and she's right. I can see part of the school, but no parking lot, no gym doors. Then I swing back around and notice the light from the top floor of Mr. Ron's house. "Maybe from the second story?"

"Well, I didn't see anything 'cause I went to bed early. Ron stayed out late with his buddy, Mr. Brick."

"You mean Mr. Mason," I suggest.

"Brick, stone, mason, the one who uses bricks for his driveway. Ron would have told the cops or that fancy new principal if he'd seen that VW hit the gym doors." She puffs smoke out from around the cigar. The smell strikes me as herbal campfire. The end of her cigar glows and her eyes narrow again. "You sure you two aren't running away from home? Or prowling to do some break-ins?"

"Just the opposite," Renée answers, and I elbow her.

What if Mr. Ron's mom is the criminal, after all?

She puffs again. Then gestures toward the library parking lot. "A pack of raccoons hangs out around the community centre this time of night. You maybe want to hold onto those leashes real tight …"

"Oh my gosh!" Renée says as a large creature waddles across the park at that precise moment.

The dogs haven't seen it yet, but then another smaller one scrambles after it. And another.

My mouth drops open. Mistake number two of the day: I don't follow Mrs. Ron's advice quickly enough. Pong yanks the leash right out of my hands.

Ping chases after him, dragging Renée like a wagon. "Pong, Pong!" I call.

Ping barks frantically. I grab for my treat bag, but there's only liver crumble left in it.

The raccoons scramble faster. The mom dashes back toward the community centre building; the little ones scatter. Pong flies after her, across the west side of the grounds, past the skateboard park. Over Brant Street.

A car screeches to a stop.

Pong and the raccoon don't seem to notice. They disappear into the forest.

Renée and Ping and I cross over more carefully.

Rouf, rouf, rouf! Ping won't stop barking.

Unfortunately, Pong stays quiet as usual.

DAY THREE, MISTAKE THREE

A half an hour later, the mom raccoon ambles back across Brant Street. I'm happy Pong didn't hurt her, but where the heck is he? "Do you think that raccoon took Pong out?" I ask Renée.

She shakes her head. "But something else must have happened to him. Greyhounds have a keen prey response, especially the ones that race. He would never have stopped chasing her."

"You don't think he's been run over?"

"Nah, I haven't seen any cars. Have you?"

"No. Someone in the neighbourhood must have taken Pong in!" I think out loud. "Let's circle the block just to make sure he's not hanging around somewhere."

Ping likes this suggestion and pulls hard, quiet for a change, but steel-locomotive determined.

As we round the bend, Ping slumps down, giving a long drawn-out whine. I know how he feels. Renée frowns and sighs. "It's late. We should go home."

"And abandon Pong?"

"Haven't you read *The Incredible Journey*? Animals travel amazing distances to get home."

"What if he gets run over on the way?"

"Not that many cars this time of night, and he's a big enough dog to see. Maybe he's already sitting outside his house right now."

"What if he's not?"

"Then tomorrow we can knock on every door. It's too late now; people would call the police on us." She stoops down to pat Ping and talks softly as if to comfort him, too. "We'll post signs on poles.

We'll visit the animal shelter. We'll find him, don't worry." She gives me hope.

"Fine, you're right. Let's go home."

But Ping balks at moving. Mule dog digs his paws in each time Renée pulls at the leash. "Pong's gone home," she tells him as she picks him up. "We have to go, too."

We pass the strip mall before Ping finally settles. The yellow CLOSED sign glows in the window at the pizza place, which reminds me. "After I noticed all the toilet paper decorating Mrs. Watier's house, I saw Mr. Sawyer here. Did you know he lives in this part of the neighbourhood?"

"Yeah, I always wondered how he could afford it."

"Endorsements from when he was Mr. Universe, I bet. What I forgot to mention is that I saw a piece of single-ply stuck to his back."

We cross Brant. "You have the best observation skills of anyone I know," Renée says as we head to my street. "So Mr. Sawyer toilet-papered Mrs. Watier's house. Do you think he put something in her gas tank, too?"

"He could have. Mr. Ron and I saw him speed away in the Beetle just before I met you near the library yesterday morning."

"Is this all about him having to transfer?" Renée sounds doubtful as she turns to me, which forces me to think about it more.

"You're right, it can't be. We know they went out over the summer. Even if he hadn't mopped her down, she probably needed to transfer him to stop gossip."

"It's awfully quick for her to plan a wedding to a different guy, though."

"You're right. That might make me drive a car into a school."

"Did he think it would stop her marriage, somehow?"

"I don't know. Maybe he did it 'cause he's just plain mad at her."

We're at the Bennetts' house by now. There's no dog sitting on the front porch. I check the side and the back, just in case. I call out his name softly so as not to wake the neighbours. Nothing. I groan. "Where are you, Pong?"

Ping whimpers.

Renée shrugs. "Maybe he's at your house."

Exhausted and discouraged, we trudge the final block and see no greyhound at my house, either. Just for my own peace of mind, I peek into the Lebels' yard and pool. No dog swimming or running. We go inside and tiptoe upstairs. Renée heads for the guest room. Ping follows me onto my bed. I'm certain I won't get any rest that way, so I close my eyes and sigh. But I'm wrong.

Mistake number three of the day — thinking I'll stay up all night worrying — is easily the best one.

Next time I open my eyes, it's time to get up, and the half-chime of my cell sounds. I have a message from M.Y.O.B.

You were looking for trouble so I took the dog.

Fingers of ice walk up my spine. Nooooo! I thumb-key back quickly: *We just walked Ping and Pong. They had the runs.* I wait for a few moments. Don't hurt Pong, don't hurt Pong.

The half-chime rings again. *If you want to see your dog again, you will deliver $500 in unmarked bills. Don't tell anyone!*

It's like a bad dream, combined with every kidnap movie I've ever seen. What are unmarked bills, anyway? I've always wondered. Do I need to make sure I get money that's really clean looking?

I need proof he's alive, I type. It's what all the detectives and agents ask for in these kidnap stories.

At the next chime, Renée shows up at my bedroom door in her pajamas, rubbing her eyes. "What's up?"

"M.Y.O.B. is texting me. He's sent me a picture this time. Come and look at this."

Renée leans on my shoulder so she can see. The photo of Pong shows him looking all right. Underneath him is a tented piece of paper with this message on it: $500 by 5:00 today.

"What! Stall! Ask for more time," Renée suggests. "Tell him you can't possibly raise the money that fast."

"I have the money in my account. The Bennetts come back tomorrow night. We don't have more time."

Where? I type back instead.

Ding! *The bus stop on Brant and Cavendish.*

"Great!" Renée says. "Then the police will come and arrest him."

"You actually think the dognapper will bring Pong?"

The half-chime rings. *Once I get the money, I tell you where the greyhound is.*

"Wow, it's like he can hear what we're saying to each other."

I quickly look out the window but don't see anyone around. I scrunch up my face because all I want to do is yell for Mom. Not like she could help. She'd just tell me one of her crazy stories. Still, I need one of those now.

"It's okay, Stephen." Renée pats my shoulder. "This is okay, really. Pong didn't get run over. You can get the money by five o'clock. And we have till then to figure out who did it and find Pong ourselves."

DAY THREE, MISTAKE FOUR

"Kids! Wake up!" Dad's voice booms from downstairs. "Breakfast is ready!"

"Just getting dressed. We'll be down in a sec," I call back and then meet Renée in the hall. Nothing sparkles in her hair. She's wearing a T-shirt with a dog on it, jeans, and sneakers. It's the sneakers that sparkle today, and of course, her glasses.

"What will we tell him?" she asks. "He's going to want to know where Pong is."

I think for a moment. "We'll say the dogs were fighting in the middle of the night, so we separated them. Took Pong back to the Bennetts.'"

"That's good. Stick as close to the truth as possible."

I nod. "They always fight. And we were walking them past midnight."

Renée and I take turns in the bathroom, then head downstairs, Ping following at my heels.

"Good morning, Renée, Stephen," Dad says, twisting his head back from the open fridge. He seems to be moving the entire contents of the vegetable bin to the counter. Several bags and a large stockpot sit next to the piles of carrots and celery. Pancakes are stacked on the kitchen table. "Got my secret ingredients ready. Making lots of liver bites today!"

The phone rings.

"That will be your mom." He picks up and chats while Renée and I eat. "Stephen is doing a great job walking Ping and Pong," he tells her.

A twinge of guilt hits me. I lost Pong. How much worse a job could I do? Lose Ping, too?

"I have a new client," Dad continues and chats about the Yorkies. "Yes, and imagine, Mr. Mason ordered more dog treats!"

At the last word, Ping's ears flick up for a second. They sink down in a moment and he gives a little moan. Feeling sorry for him, I sneak him his own pancake, but without Pong to compete with over it, he doesn't seem interested.

"Stephen had a sleepover with a new friend. Yes, it is wonderful. Here. I'll let you speak to him." He hands me the receiver.

"Hi, Mom. Where are you?" I look down as Ping sniffs dejectedly at his treat.

"London. I'll be home tomorrow but a little late. Nice you made a new friend. Dad let you have a sleepover in the middle of the week?"

"Yeah, there were some problems at her house. She needed to get away."

"Your father didn't say it was a girl."

"Why would he? What difference does it make?" I pat Ping, and he slumps down beside his pancake, finally giving it a little lick.

"You're right. Sounds like you were just helping a friend. That's good. Hope you got enough sleep, though."

Me too, I think. Ping flips over, legs in the air.

"Got another animal story for you. Which is why I'm going to be late, by the way. It happened on our own plane!"

"Does it have a happy ending?"

"Oh, sure." She chuckles and continues. "A lady came on with her cat in a bag. She stowed it under the seat ahead of her, just the way she was supposed to."

"Did you get all stuffed up?" In which case, maybe she won't notice the dog dander when she gets home. I pat Ping's tummy now.

"My eyes are burning and I'm sniffly, thanks for asking. But get this: Ripples escaped from her bag before we could even take off."

"Ripples?"

"The name of the cat. His owner called after him as he dodged from seat to seat. We called and chased, too, but he dove into the cockpit."

"The cat didn't die, did he?"

"Happy ending, remember? So no, he didn't die. But he got in behind the instrument panel, and we couldn't get him out on our own. We tried everything, offering him a salmon tray …"

"Nobody likes airline food."

"Not Ripples, anyway." Mom and I chuckle together. "Then we had to clear the plane, and the maintenance workers removed some panels to finally get him."

"But he's okay?"

"He's a bit shook up but he wasn't injured. The mechanics are checking over the wires before we take off."

"So animals really can't travel safely at all."

Mom's voice drops. "It is better for them to stay home." Then it lifts again. "But then owners can hire people like your father to walk their dogs. Just think what a valuable service you guys are providing." Mom sounds pretty cheery about this. "Oh, they're calling me. Wires must have all checked out."

"Really? That was awful quick. Hope they did a good job."

"Ciao!"

"See you, Mom." We both hang up at the same time.

Dad smiles at me. "She'll be home soon." He grabs some bags from the counter and hands one each to Renée and me. "Your lunches. You didn't bring home your backpacks, so they're in grocery bags. Hope you like egg salad, Renée."

"Love it."

"I'm going to see the Yorkies. Lock the door behind you. I can walk Ping and Pong at noon if you like …"

"No, Dad. We'll do it, no worries." He doesn't seem to notice Pong is missing.

Once Dad's gone, we head out toward school, taking the long way so we can leave Ping at the

Bennetts'. He stays close to my heels the whole way. That training session paid off big-time. Mind you, he also seems very interested in my lunch. When he nips at the bag, I have to push him down and scold him. "Bad dog, that's egg salad. Not for you." But otherwise, he really behaves.

"So after school we'll go to the bank to get the money," I tell Renée.

"You have enough?"

"Yes, but I don't know what the withdrawal limit is. I've never taken that much out before."

"I'll bring the coins from my piggy bank, just in case."

"Thanks."

At school we head for our lockers, but then we spot Bruno and Tyson in the hall.

"Hey, Green Lantern." Tyson points at my leg. "What happened?"

"You're bleeding all over the place," Bruno says.

Finally I look down and realize that Dad made an accidental switcheroo this morning. I should have known something was up when Ping nipped at the bag. I should have checked then. My mistake, number four of the day. Everyone's staring at me. I'm not going to live this one down till I go to college, either.

DAY THREE, MISTAKE FIVE

I stand frozen as a crowd gathers. Mrs. Watier spots the commotion and strides up to me, *click-click,* in her tall-heeled boots. She gasps when she sees my jeans and quickly drags me into her office. Renée slips in behind before she shuts the door.

"How did you get hurt?" Mrs. Watier asks.

"Oh, no, this isn't *my* blood. My father accidentally switched my lunch for a bag of beef liver."

Mrs. Watier tilts her head.

"He was defrosting it to make treats for his dog-walking clients, but he packed my lunch in the same type of bag."

Mrs. Watier still looks confused but nods. "I should call your mother. Maybe she can pick you up."

"My mother is in London right now. You might reach my dad on his cell, but he can't just drop everything, so it could be a while." She keeps nodding so I continue. "I can walk myself. I live really close by. If I can just get some extra plastic bags to carry the liver, I'll go home to change." When Dad gets back from the Yorkies, he's going to need this bag of meat, I think.

"Can I go home with Stephen to make sure he's all right?" Renée asks. She makes it seem as though that blood on my leg is seeping from a wound.

Mrs. Watier stares down at me and frowns.

The jeans stick to my leg now, and I tug the denim away from my skin. I certainly don't need looking after, but on the other hand, I want Renée's company for what I have planned.

"That might be a good idea." She reaches behind her into a cabinet and pulls out a couple of bags for me.

As she turns back, I notice some photos propped up on that cabinet. One is of a young boy who looks familiar. Something strange about his eyes. They look almost crossed. "Is that your son?" I ask.

"Yes. He's older now, goes to Champlain High." She picks up the phone and asks for my father's number.

I tell her and she dials it.

Then it hits me. It's him, the skateboarder, the boy with the two different-coloured eyes.

"He's not picking up."

"Mrs. Watier, I need to go home to change. He won't mind. You have his permission note for me to leave the property."

"You have one for me, too," Renée chimes in.

"Do you have human food?" she asks Renée. "Or dog liver?"

Renée checks her bag and legs. "No dripping here," she answers. "Can I please keep him company, anyway?"

"Very well." Mrs. Watier sighs. "Go with him but hurry back. You know they're having a special assembly soon."

"The one to celebrate your marriage?" Renée asks.

Mrs. Watier nods and winks. "I'm not supposed to know, but there's going to be cake."

"Don't forget to give Mrs. Klein a piece," I tell her. "The custodial staff like to be included, too."

"Don't be weird," Renée grumbles into my ear as she yanks me away. "We'll hurry," she agrees out loud for Mrs. Watier's benefit.

We make a quick dash down the hall, so we don't get any more gasps or stares.

But once we're outside the school building, I slow down and tell Renée my plan. "Let's stop to get Ping first, then drop the liver off and I'll change. Afterwards, I'd like to make a visit to your house."

"Why?" She stops walking.

"You can get your piggy bank, for one thing."

"You really just want to check Attila's bookshelf," Renée snaps. "You still don't believe he's innocent."

"I can't take chances when it concerns Pong's life."

Renée digs her fists into her hips. "You think he's hiding a greyhound at our house?"

"No. But Ping will go crazy sniffing if he's been anywhere near Attila."

"Well, he hasn't been."

"Okay. But I still need to ask your brother some questions."

She crosses her arms and frowns at me.

"Come on, Renée. You know how I read stuff into things. If I can be sure he's innocent, the rest of the world will, too. I will find the real criminal and prove it to the police."

"Fine." Her arms are still folded but we continue walking.

At the Bennetts' house, Ping's bark sounds like a strangled yelp, and when we open the door, he whimpers instead of barks. "You missing Pong, boy? It's okay, we're going to get him today." At least I hoped so.

We snap him to the leash easily and lock up the Bennetts' house again. We run up the street to my house, where I change and then swap the liver for the bag with an egg salad sandwich.

I bring the bloody jeans downstairs and pour some stain remover onto the spots. Then we set out again.

"Ping really wants to go the other way," Renée says.

"Well, he can't. After school we can come back and give him his full walk. I'll go to the bank for the rest of the money, and we can take him wherever he wants to go. For now, carry him if he doesn't want to come."

She lifts him up and we keep walking. When he gets heavy, I take a turn; then when I get tired, too, I make him walk again. "You need your exercise," I tell Ping. "You're not helping Pong by moping." Finally, we're at Renée's house. To be honest, I'm not even sure what I'll ask Attila. I'm just counting on Ping's reaction to tell us everything.

"Attila, are you home?" Renée calls.

"Whad'ya want," a voice comes from the basement.

We follow it down. No reaction from Ping at all. He doesn't push to get ahead. I have to drag him. No scent of Pong, then. It's definite.

At the bottom of the stairs, I'm shocked at how neat Attila's room is. The bed looks smooth with fuchsia-coloured sheets tucked in and the matching duvet draped perfectly over. Books line up in a straight row on a shelf — pine planks on brick. All of the bricks appear to be in place. From one wall, a huge print dominates. I stare at it. On it a maid with a broom and dustpan lifts a blanket to reveal a brick wall.

"Do you not recognize the picture?" Renée asks me. "It's a Banksy print."

I shake my head. "Who is Banksy?"

"Only the world's best-known graffiti artist," Attila growls. He's sitting at a large black desk. We interrupted him sketching. "What are you doing in my bedroom?"

"We wanted to ask you something," Renée says.

"Do you know a skateboarder with two different-coloured eyes?" I jump in. "He goes to your high school."

"Don't know him that well. But I've seen him around, sure."

"He's Mrs. Watier's son," Renée tells him.

"Who's Mrs. Watier and why should I care?"

"She's our new principal. She's getting married this weekend," I explain.

"So?" he grumbles.

"We think the whole car-in-the-wall thing may be related to her wedding. Someone wants to mess it up for her."

"The kid with the weird eyes? I heard him tell someone he's going to Montreal. Is the wedding in Montreal?"

"No. The wedding's right here in town, I over-heard. The Royal Botanical Gardens," Renée says.

"The custodian!" Attila suddenly says.

"What?" Renée asks.

"The new blond custodian got into a shov-ing match with Mr. Moody. Something about a wedding."

"Mr. Sawyer!" I agree. "He toilet papered Mrs. Watier's house." Mistake number five of the day is that we leap along to Attila's conclusion, which is that Mr. Sawyer is the vandal and therefore

M.Y.O.B. After all, why would Mr. Sawyer need five hundred dollars?

DAY THREE, MISTAKE SIX

It feels really awful leaving Ping alone again at the Bennetts' when he's so unhappy about his missing pal. I hear his whimpering in my head as we rush the rest of the way to the school. We check in at the office, which is crowded with all kinds of strangers holding plates of cake in their hands.

I'm guessing the tall dark-haired guy with the tuxedo T-shirt labelled GROOM is Mr. Moody. He has a goatee and black eyebrows that shoot away from his forehead in pointed arrows. The beard and eyebrows make him look like a magician or a wizard. Maybe he bewitched Mrs. Watier into marrying him. That would explain a lot.

Mrs. Watier must have even invited Mr. Mason in from his work on the damaged wall of the school. He's standing with his plate just outside the office door.

"We missed the assembly," Renée says.

"But not the refreshments." I smile.

"If you want a piece of cake, you can head to the gym," Mrs. Watier calls to us.

"Don't you want to tell her who the vandal is?" Renée asks as we leave the office.

"Shhh! Keep your voice down!" I say but it's too late. The half-chime on my phone sounds. I check my messages.

M.Y.O.B. *Keep your mouth shut or say goodbye to Pong.*

I squeeze my eyes closed tight and feel Renée's hand on my shoulder. "It's almost over. We'll get Pong back, don't worry," she says gently.

I open my eyes and, oh my gosh, there he is. "Renée, look, Mr. Sawyer's going into the gym!"

"Well, let's follow."

We hustle after our former custodian and stand several kids behind him in line for cake. Mr. Ron is there, too, trusty stop sign and cap tucked under his armpit. He looks different without his hat; his hair looks flattened, and across his forehead is a wide, grey mark. A cap line?

I reach in my back pocket for my phone.

"What are you doing?" Renée asks me.

"I'm dialing M.Y.O.B. He just texted me, so if it's Mr. Sawyer, something will ring on him. I hold up the phone so Renée can listen in. We hear the chain of blips, and then I listen for a telltale ring of some kind.

Nothing makes a noise on Mr. Sawyer as he moves up to get his slice. He doesn't stop to reach into his pockets, either.

I hang up.

We watch him head to the office and spot Mrs. Klein, sipping a coffee on the bench at the side of the gym, an empty plate beside her. René and I walk over to her.

"You got invited," I say.

Mrs. Klein just smiles. "Good cake, too, not too sweet. I hate it when the icing is a solid brick of butter and sugar."

"Really, eh?" Her icing description makes me suddenly think of something. "Mrs. Klein, you saw the brick that was on the accelerator. Did you tell reporters it was red?"

"Yes, it was kind of a rusty red, though. Old looking, you know?"

"Did it have a dent in the middle?" Renée asks.

"Yeah."

"Did it have the word *Standard* stamped across it?" I add.

"Uh-huh. I never paid attention to bricks before, but that's exactly what it looked like."

"Thanks!" Renée and I chime out together. We dash back to the main office. Just outside the door, Mr. Mason's still standing there, finishing his cake.

"Mrs. Watier, could you come here?" Renée calls.

Inside the office, Mrs. Watier touches Mr. Moody's elbow as she leans in to whisper something in his ear. He nods and she steps out the door to join us.

Mr. Mason heads to the bin with his empty cake plate.

"No, please stay, Mr. Mason," I grab his arm as he moves toward the exit. "This concerns you, too."

"I should get back to work," he grumbles.

"Mrs. Watier," I start when she joins us, "the brick that was on the accelerator of the Beetle came from Mr. Mason's special supply."

"He told us that he keeps strict inventory because they are reclaimed," Renée continues.

"He insisted that none of them were stolen," I add.

We make our sixth mistake of the day as I finish. "Therefore, we conclude that Mr. Mason was the one who drove that car into the school building using one of his special reclaimed bricks. He wanted the work."

DAY THREE, MISTAKE SEVEN

"That's ridiculous," Mr. Mason sputters. "I get jobs based on quality workmanship. I don't commit crimes to get them. If you ask me —" His muttering gets interrupted as Mr. Ron strolls toward us.

"Hey, kids! Hey, George!" He holds one huge hand up in a stop-sign hello. The other hand holds onto his plate of cake. "Never met a frosting that I didn't like." He takes a forkful in his mouth and grins a pink-icing smile. His grin drops as he sees the angry look on Mr. Mason's face.

"Just because nobody stole any of my bricks," Mr. Mason continues, "doesn't mean I vandalized the school. I gave one to Ronnie here. He wanted it for an ashtray for his mom. Ya don't see me accusing him of that car crash because of it."

"Yup, yup."

On a sudden inspiration, I reach up and touch the grey mark across Mr. Ron's forehead.

"Ow! Stop!" He ducks away.

"That's a strange bruise," I say. "It's shaped almost like a steering wheel."

We all turn to stare at Mr. Ron, who wipes his mouth with a sleeve.

"You never gave your mother that ashtray," Renée pipes in. "You bought her a glass one yesterday. We saw it."

Mrs. Watier and Mr. Mason both turn to Mr. Ron, waiting for a logical explanation.

"Yup, yup. Thought she'd like a reclaimed brick. Old and tough, just like her. But she didn't."

"What did you do with the brick, then?" I ask.

"Um, um, don't really remember …" His face turns blotchy red.

"When did you give him the brick?" Renée asks Mr. Mason.

"Geez, I don't know. Started working on that wall Monday ... yeah, that's it, had to be Monday night."

"And did he leave your house around midnight?" I ask.

Mr. Mason squints at Mr. Ron now. "Around then, yeah."

"So he left, carrying the brick, probably walked past the school and saw the Beetle in the parking lot," I say.

"But why did you put the brick on the accelerator to drive it into the school?" Renée asks.

"I never put that brick on the accelerator to drive the Beetle into the school."

"Yeah, some punk must have done it," Mr. Mason says. "What d'ya do with the brick, Buddy?"

"Did your mother put it on the accelerator?" I ask. "She doesn't have it anymore, does she?"

"Maw would never ..." I expect him to keep denying everything, but instead he crumbles. "I ... I ... I didn't put the brick on to crash the Bug into the school on purpose. Just like you said, I saw the Beetle that night all on its own in the parking lot. No one was around. I just wanted to peek to see if the interior had changed. I love Beetles."

"You learned to drive in one," I add.

"Not very well," he says. "Whoever drove that car there left the keys in the ignition. I'm not a criminal or anything. I just wanted to give it a spin for old times' sake."

"You drove the Beetle?" Mr. Mason asks.

"Yeah, perfectly! But then, when I went to park it, I accidentally gave 'er gas and it slammed it into the school."

"You crashed it? You're lucky you weren't hurt," Mrs. Watier says.

"Then you put your Mom's birthday present on the accelerator to make it look like vandalism?" I ask.

Mr. Ron rolls his head from side to side as though he wants to deny it. But finally, he can't. "I didn't want everyone to know what a bad driver I am. So I turned the ignition again and put the brick on the pedal. I never meant to get any one else in trouble. I hoped the school would get a new gym. That it would all work out."

"You said you weren't a criminal. Yet you dognapped Pong and asked for a ransom. Where are you keeping him?" Renée asks.

Mr. Ron furrows his brow. He looks genuinely confused. "Is that one of the dogs you were walking the other day?" he asks.

"Yes. What did you do with him?" I ask with as firm a voice as I can muster.

"Nothing, I swear."

I dig my fists into my hips and try to stare him down. One of my fists must have grazed the screen of my phone. We hear the telltale *blip, blip, blip* of a dialing cellphone. It doesn't hit me what I've done, my standard mistake, pocket calling the last person I dialed. Number seven for today. But it's the best mistake I've ever made because suddenly, we hear the faint ringing coming from Mrs. Watier's office.

DAY THREE, MISTAKE EIGHT

Mrs. Watier doesn't look alarmed, nor does she rush to answer it.

"Whose phone is that?" I ask.

"What? What phone?" She tilts her head.

"The one ringing from your office," Renée tells her. "Stephen has been getting threatening phone calls from it."

With everyone quiet, Mrs. Watier hears the ring this time. "Serge? Is that you in there? Why don't you come out and join everyone?"

"Is Serge your son?" Renée asks.

"Yes, he is. The staff invited him to the assembly as well."

"I accidentally redialed the last number that contacted me. The person on the other end dognapped my client and is holding him hostage."

"What client?"

"A greyhound I walk. His name is Pong."

"I think I might know if Serge was hiding a

greyhound in the house. Serge!" she calls. "Serge, you need to come out here."

No answer.

"Didn't you have the VW Bug in your driveway Monday evening?" Renée asks Mrs. Watier. "You drove it to your wedding dress fitting."

"Serge had the opportunity to steal the Beetle, that's for sure," I agree. "I heard that someone put something in your TZX's gas tank that afternoon." My mind is spinning now and I think out loud: "Maybe it was to prevent you from getting to that fitting!"

"Mrs. Watier, does your son like the idea of you remarrying?" I ask her. "'Cause I saw him the night of your wedding dress fitting. He looked pretty mad."

"Why would he threaten the school?" she asks.

"If he really hates the idea of your marriage, I think he'd do anything to cause a hitch in your plans," I answer.

"Serge would have access to the computer lab at Champlain High — that's where the bomb threat came from," Renée says.

"I don't believe it. I mean, I know he's not happy with me remarrying. But all that seems so drastic."

"He told his friends he was going to Montreal this weekend. Does he have the money to get there? The dognapper demanded five hundred dollars for the return of my greyhound client."

The last detail twigs something in Mrs. Watier. She turns white. "My ex-husband lives in Montreal. Serge!" She screams the name this time. When she marches toward the office, the skateboarding dude suddenly appears, weaving from behind the counter, pushing past her and us.

"Stupid wedding!" he curses. Then he yells out. "You'll never see that greyhound again." He races down the hall and out the door.

"You must believe us now," I tell her as I walk toward the door. "Can you call the police?"

"Where are you going?" Mrs. Watier asks. "You can't leave the building. School isn't over yet."

"It's a matter of life and death. We have to save Pong. The greyhound," I add so she understands. "C'mon Renée." I grab her arm and tug her along. "Hurry," I tell her, "or they'll stop us."

We run through the halls, push through the double doors, and burst on to the playground.

"Where to first?" Renée asks.

"We're going to do what we should have done right from the start. We're springing Ping and letting him lead the way."

And here's the eighth mistake we make that day. Neither one of us thinks to call my dad in for backup.

DAY THREE, MISTAKE NINE

My hand trembles as I insert the key into the Bennetts' lock. I want to hurry so badly that I overturn it, unlocking and then accidentally locking the door again. Ack, mistake number nine of the day!

Yes, Mom, crashing a plane would be worse, I think, *but this mistake is annoying, too.*

"Here, let me." Renée turns the key once smoothly and then pushes open the door.

Ping rushes us but doesn't mess around jumping up and nipping my butt as he usually does. I snap on the leash, and then we're back outside again. "We're going to head across Brant," I explain to Renée as we jog, Ping in the lead. "That's where we lost Pong in the first place."

"And that's where Serge lives."

"Exactly!"

"Only, Mrs. Watier didn't hear or see Pong in her house," Renée says.

"Pong is the quietest dog I've ever known, toenails excepting. And Mrs. Watier's house is big."

"A greyhound is big, too."

"It was near their house that Ping slumped down last night. Remember he didn't want to go anywhere and you had to pick him up?"

Right now the little dog churns forward like a locomotive. Determined, on a mission. He never stops to pee once. On the other side of the street, the lady in the lime gym suit walks Buddy the Rottweiler. She calls hello and waves, but Ping doesn't even turn his head.

We cross Brant, past the forest. Something rattles in the bushes. A squirrel? Another raccoon? Ping will never know, as he hurtles forward without even a sideways sniff. As we draw closer to the final curve in the street, I realize we have no plan. "What are we going to do? Break into the house?"

"Drop his leash. Maybe Ping will sniff out what part of the house Pong is in."

"Last time we let Ping loose, he knocked Serge over, remember?"

"We can only hope," Renée answers.

She has a point. I completely unhitch Ping.

He begins to bark like a maniac, tearing up the path to Jessie's old house, only now, of course, Mrs. Watier and Serge live there.

Instead of beelining to the door, he swerves and dashes to the side gate. There, he starts digging frantically. The earth sprays behind him.

"Here, Ping, let me." I reach over the gate to unlatch it and then push it open. The dog tears around the pool and heads directly for the pool house.

Jessie's and my old playhouse.

Ping scratches frantically at the front door. I try the doorknob. It's locked. The sound of Ping's claws is so loud I can't hear myself think. Then, I realize, it's not just Ping's toenails.

I move a patio chair over to the small, high window, stand on it, and peer in. "Oh, Pong. Poor boy. We're here for you. We'll get you out of there. Don't you worry."

"How are you going to get him out?" Renée asks.

"Well, we could break this window with the pool hook hanging on the fence, but Jessie used to keep a key under the planter over there."

Renée beats me to the flowerpot and lifts it up. "Check!" She holds a key in her hand.

I grab it from her and stick it in the doorknob. This time I turn the key smoothly. I open the door and Pong bursts out.

Ping and Pong greet each other like mismatched best friends. Ping licks at Pong's snout. Pong puts his large paw on Ping's back. Ping slides out from Pong's paw and jumps on his back. Pong gives Ping's paw a friendly nibble and Ping snaps back.

Suddenly, they're growling and snapping at each other just like old times. I separate them and pat Pong at the same time.

"We should get going before Serge Watier finds us here," Renée suggests.

Renée's right. She's always right.

DAY THREE, MISTAKE TEN

Mistake number ten is that we don't move out of there quickly enough. As we turn to leave, we find Serge blocking our way. He's holding on to the end of his skateboard, swinging it like a baseball bat.

"You're not going anywhere with that dog unless you hand over five hundred dollars," he says.

"Do you take debit?" I ask.

Serge scowls and slams the skateboard against the fence.

"I guess not. How much did you bring, Renée?"

"Thirteen dollars and twenty-five cents," she answers.

"That's not enough!" Serge growls. "I have to pay for a train ticket."

"Listen, my mother can get you a plane ticket for way less. You have to go standby but …"

"Shut up!"

"Come on, Serge," Renée reasons, "even if you get the money, your mom knows where you're heading. Unless you change your mind and live on the street instead of your dad's."

"You shut up, too." Serge slams his skateboard against the fence a second time. This time there's a loud *crack*.

I grab Renée's hand and force her to back up with me. We block the dogs from Serge.

"Step away," he growls. "I'm taking the big one."

"I won't let you hurt Pong. I'll get you the money."

"I'd never hurt Pong. He's the only dog I've ever had. I'm taking him with me. We'll hitchhike."

"Well … that could work," I stall. Over the top of the gate, I see a blond head and dare to hope. I turn to Renée and twitch my eyebrow to signal her. The latch rattles. Serge looks behind him, and Renée and I dive for his legs. He falls on top of us, but I scramble to snap up the skateboard first.

Mr. Sawyer grabs Serge by the T-shirt. It bunches in his hand as he lifts him up. Serge flails but the T-shirt stays tucked in Mr. S's fist. "First, I catch you messing up the house with toilet paper. And I go along with it 'cause I know you're upset. I figure you need to let off steam. But this? Where does it end with you?"

"She dumped you, too! How can you let her marry that guy!"

"Because I love her and I know it will make her happy."

Aw, I think.

Maybe Serge starts to feel the same way. He stops struggling. His strangely coloured eyes fill up. I can see it's hard for him not to cry.

Now I feel sorry for him instead of scared.

In the distance I hear a siren; it's drawing nearer. Mrs. Watier or someone must have called the police. Finally, I fix mistake number eight. I reach for my cellphone. "I'm calling my father. You should call home, too, Renée. Your parents will be happy to hear your brother is off the hook."

When Dad answers, I give him a shortened version of everything that's happened, starting with the Pong dognap.

He's stunned. I can tell because he really has no comments, nothing to say that I've over-analyzed or over-thought anything. Nothing to put things in a way sunnier light. "I'm just taking the liver bites out of the oven. I'll be there in five minutes," he says and hangs up.

The police arrive before him and cuff Serge's hands behind his back.

Mrs. Watier walks through the gate moments later, no future groom in sight. She gasps when she spots her son and those handcuffs. She rushes over and hugs Serge. I wonder whether she wants to slug him, too.

Renée and I tell the dognapping story all over again, and the officer gives us her card. "We'll need to take your statements at the station later, with a parent present."

Ping and Pong wrestle with each other. Now that they're over being happy to see each other, they need a walk.

Dad pushes through the gate as the police lead Serge away. I can smell cooked liver.

Mr. Sawyer follows them out.

"Wow," Dad says, "you guys solved the crime." In his hand is a bag of fresh dog treats. Ping and Pong immediately sit quiet and tall. Ping even holds his paw out.

I smile, happy that it's all over.

"Renée, I can give you a lift home. Or do you want to go back to school?" Dad asks.

"I'd really like to walk the dogs with Stephen."

"So, you don't want a lift, either?" he asks me. "You don't want to go back to class?"

"No!" I shake my head.

"So you don't need me at all?" Dad says.

"Oh, yes, I do!" I take two steps and reach my arms around him for a hug. He hugs me back. "I'll take those dog treats, too."

He hands over the bag. "You could have told me all this was happening to you. I can't believe you dealt with it all on your own."

"It was a mistake, I'll admit that. But it turned out okay, which is the important thing. And it's not even the worst mistake I made. It's certainly not as bad as forgetting to put the landing gear down and doing a belly dive with an airplane.

"And if the kids at school hear that we found the person who crashed the car into the school, maybe when I get to university they will remember me for solving that crime, instead of dropping my drawers when I had no gym shorts underneath ... or shouting fire when there really wasn't one ... or bringing raw beef liver for lunch."

"You're over-thinking this, Stephen," Renée says.

"It's one of my worst flaws," I admit.

"But it's your best quality, too. Who else would have figured out that brick connection?"

Who else keeps accidentally butt-dialing people? I have to admit, some of my worst mistakes lead to something interesting.

the
aftermath

THE GREAT MISTAKE
MYSTERIES

Mom comes home late the next night. Right away, she's red-eyed and all stuffed up.

Busted! But how could the dog dander cause her to react so quickly? "Sorry, Mom. We kept Ping and Pong here for a couple of nights. I vacuumed everywhere they could have been."

"Mrs. Bennett texted me about the great job you did watching her dogs." Mom peers around as she hangs up her coat. "The house looks good." She points to her eyes and circles her finger to her nose. "This is from the hearing dog we had on our flight. We have to allow service dogs in the cabin."

"Poor you. Let me make you a tea," Dad says.

"I gave the owner your business card," Mom says as she follows him into the kitchen. "He lives on Overton."

"What a coincidence," Dad says.

I tag along behind them into the kitchen. "Mom, I have to tell you everything that happened with Ping and Pong and with the car that drove into the school."

"Okay. I'm a little hungry. Do you have anything around to eat?"

"Liver bites! They're such a big hit. Mom, even Mr. Mason bought some."

She grins. "Yeah, but I hate liver."

"Let me make you some peanut butter apple," I suggest.

We sit at the table and she helps me cut up the fruit. Dad spreads the peanut butter on them and Mom and I share.

"Mmm," Mom says and sighs. "Go ahead, tell me."

"Well, it turns out the principal's son Serge sent the bomb scare email to his own mother."

"Wow. He must have really wanted her attention."

"Yeah, he didn't want her to marry his shop teacher," I explain. "He put something in her gas tank so she wouldn't be able to get to her wedding dress fitting. But instead she borrowed the car his shop class was working on."

"The Beetle?" Mom asks.

"Yes. When he saw it in the driveway, he grabbed the keys and took off with it. He abandoned it in the school parking lot. Just trying to throw another hitch into her plans."

"I heard she's actually postponing the wedding now," Dad says.

"Who told you that?" I look at him.

"Oh, I chatted with Mr. Sawyer at the grocery store. He seemed pretty happy about that, too."

"Anyway," I continue, "Serge is not the one who drove the car into the school. Our crossing guard did that."

"Not the nice man who's been your crossing guard since forever?" Mom asks.

"Yup, yup," I answer, imitating Mr. Ron. "He loves Volkswagens and when he noticed it sitting there with the keys in the ignition, he couldn't resist taking it for a spin. Only he can't drive very well. He doesn't even have a license."

"But that wouldn't matter if he just drove it on private property," Dad says.

"Except that he crashed it into the school by accident," I say. "Probably the second-worst mistake he's made in his life."

"Oh, dear. Was he hurt?"

"No. But the first worst mistake he made was that he didn't report it. Instead, he started up the car again, leaving a brick on the accelerator so that it would look like vandalism."

"Won't he go to jail for that?" Mom asks.

"I don't think so," Dad says. "He's offered to pay for the damage, and Mr. Mason's letting him fix the wall with him. Mrs. Watier will try to get the charges reduced to reckless driving."

"Only he can't be our crossing guard anymore." I sigh.

Mom sips at her tea and frowns. "Maybe it was time for a change, anyway."

Dad nods. "They've already replaced him. A nice lady with black hair and dark sunglasses."

"But all that's not even the worst part of the story," I continue.

"There's more?" Mom asks.

"Yes. Serge kidnapped one of the Bennetts' dogs. Pong, the greyhound."

"Oh my gosh. Did you tell them?"

"Of course. We had to," Dad says. "But Stephen rescued him, so they're very happy with us."

"Serge wanted five hundred dollars so he could run away to his father's in Montreal. Mom, he was threatening to hurt Pong."

"Well, I hope he faces some serious consequences," she says.

"Mr. Sawyer told me he would probably just get a community service sentence. He has no priors. Mrs. Watier's hoping he can serve it at an animal shelter," Dad says.

"What!" I gasp.

"It's a new program. Nurturing animals helps troubled kids feel better about themselves. And Serge really liked Pong. He never would have hurt him. He just needed to make you think he would, to get your money."

"How do you know that?"

"Mr. Sawyer." Dad shrugs. "He actually tried to take an interest in Serge when he was going out with Mrs. Watier."

"I'm very proud of you, Stephen." Mom smiles

and pats my shoulder. "I have a little story to tell you. Nothing to top yours, though."

"It doesn't involve pilot error, does it?"

"No, actually it involves a flight attendant's mistake. Friend of mine. You remember Jeannie? Red hair? No? Anyway, she missed her flight from New York back to Toronto because of it."

"What happened?" I ask.

"She decided she'd take the subway downtown because she wanted to absorb the local culture — we never have a lot of time at these layovers, so she was cutting it close, anyway — when these two kittens jumped onto the track …"

"No, no, Mom!" I cover my ears.

"Relax, Stephen. I love animals, too, you know. I gave that dog on the flight my piece of chicken." Her nose honks as she blows it again. "Just because they make my eyes weep and my nose run doesn't mean I'm going to tell you awful stories about them. Does an animal ever die in any of my stories?"

"No. That's true. Go ahead."

"Okay, well. A subway worker tries to grab them, but these two little kittens make a break for it. The transit authorities have to shut the power 'cause the third rail carries 600 volts. No one can run along it if that's on. Which meant six miles of track between stations were closed for an hour and a half."

"So what happened?" I ask.

"Like I said, she missed her flight."

"To the cats, I mean. Did they rescue them?"

"Well, yes. Six hours later the kittens returned to the same spot where they were first spotted, and that same worker caught them."

"But the trains were only shut for ninety minutes."

"You're over-thinking this. The kittens are safe. Maybe they used up some of their nine lives."

"And Pong and Ping are home, too," Dad continues. "No bombs exploded at the school."

"Only a backpack."

"Speaking of redheads, I have a crazy story, too," Dad says. "I saw the strangest thing when I was walking Buddy through Brant Hills."

"Is Buddy a Rottweiler?" I ask.

"Yeah. New client."

"I gave his owner our card," I tell him.

"Yes, thanks. Great job. Anyhow, I see this tall red-haired kid walking a chubby little Pomeranian, and when the dog squats to do his business, the kid scoops it into a bag and puts the bag in the tree."

"You're kidding. I've put his poop bag in the trash for him before," I say, although I really put it in the recycling bin. "Didn't know Red was doing it, though."

"So get this," Dad says. "I called him out on it, and he explained that he likes to ride through later on his bike and grab the poop bags from the branches to put in the trash. Sort of a sport for him. Like a knight jousting."

"Jousting for dog doo. That explains a lot. I'll have to tell Renée."

"Renée, that's the girl you had the sleepover with? Wasn't she the one you found so annoying before? You called her … wait a minute … Princess Einstein, right?" Mom asks.

"Yeah, she's really smart."

"But that's what you didn't like about her."

"Maybe it was more that I thought she was showing off all the time about it. But I was wrong, Mom. She just can't help herself. She has to share everything she knows. Blurts it out, really. She helped me walk the dogs and solve the crime, after all.

"Anyhow, she doesn't annoy me anymore. That was just me not understanding her … a mistake. Probably the worst one I made all month."

ACKNOWLEDGEMENTS

A special bombs away goes out to Staff Sergeant Glenn Mannella of the Halton Regional Police Service Emergency Services Unit, who took the time to show me his way-cool equipment, including his remote control robot, and also share a couple of his stories with me.

SOME PEOPLE COUNT THEIR BLESSINGS, BUT STEPHEN NOBLE COUNTS HIS MISTAKES.

THE GREAT MISTAKE MYSTERIES

BY SYLVIA MCNICOLL

BOOK 1

THE BEST MISTAKE MYSTERY

SYLVIA MCNICOLL

IS IT A MISTAKE TO GIVE IN TO DOGNAPPERS?

BOOK 2

THE ARTSY MISTAKE MYSTERY

SYLVIA MCNICOLL

ART IS MISSING FROM THE NEIGHBOURHOOD. HELP STEPHEN AND RENÉE CATCH THE CRIMINAL.

BOOK 3

THE Snake MISTAKE MYSTERY

SYLVIA MCNICOLL

CAN STEPHEN AND RENÉE SOLVE THE CASE OF THE MISSING PYTHON?

THEY'RE DOGGONE GOOD MYSTERIES!